SO-AXP-166

"I am disappointed that you must rush away before we've had a chance to discuss my proposal. Perhaps we can arrange to meet again at a more convenient time?"

She licked her dry lips and told herself she was imagining the predatory gleam in his eyes. "Your Highness..." Her voice sounded strangely breathless.

"Please call me Kadir, Lexi."

The way he said her name, with that soft huskiness in his voice, was too intimate, as if he had stroked each syllable with his tongue.

Lexi felt as though she was drowning in his molten gaze, but a tiny part of her sanity remained and asked why she was letting him get to her. He was a notorious womanizer, and in the past when other men like him had tried to come on to her she'd had no trouble shooting them down.

Of course she would not allow herself to be seduced by the sultan, she assured herself. But she could not deny that his interest was flattering and a salve to her wounded pride. Without conscious thought she swayed toward Kadir, bringing her mouth even closer to his. Her heart pounded and her eyelashes swept down as she waited, tense with anticipation, for him to brush his lips over hers.

Dear Reader,

Sisters often share a special bond of love and friendship—as I do with my own. I am fascinated by this unique relationship and decided to write a duet featuring two sisters.

However, when I thought of Lexi, the heroine of *Sheikh's Forbidden Conquest*, I realized that her relationship with her younger sister, Athena, was complicated because Lexi had been adopted when she was a child. A year later, her adoptive parents had a much-longed-for daughter of their own and made it clear to Lexi that they preferred Athena.

Lexi demonstrated her bravery as an RAF pilot flying rescue missions in Afghanistan. Sparks fly when she goes to work for sultan Kadir Al Sulaimar in his desert kingdom of Zenhab. The cultural differences between them are just one barrier they face, and they know they must resist the sizzling chemistry that ignites whenever they are near each other!

In the second book, shy Athena wishes she was as confident as her fiery sister. Athena was named after the Greek goddess of wisdom, but she feels she is a disappointment to her academic parents, who hoped she would follow them into a medical career.

At least her parents are pleased that she is engaged to English aristocrat Charles Fairfax. But mysterious Italian playboy Luca De Rossi has other plans for Athena!

I hope you enjoy reading about the sisters' journeys to finding true love!

Best wishes,

Chantelle

Chantelle Shaw

Sheikh's Forbidden Conquest

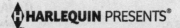
HARLEQUIN PRESENTS®

If you purchased this book without a cover you should be aware that this book is stolen property. It was reported as "unsold and destroyed" to the publisher, and neither the author nor the publisher has received any payment for this "stripped book."

Recycling programs
for this product may
not exist in your area.

ISBN-13: 978-0-373-13824-1

Sheikh's Forbidden Conquest

First North American publication 2015

Copyright © 2015 by Chantelle Shaw

All rights reserved. Except for use in any review, the reproduction or utilization of this work in whole or in part in any form by any electronic, mechanical or other means, now known or hereinafter invented, including xerography, photocopying and recording, or in any information storage or retrieval system, is forbidden without the written permission of the publisher, Harlequin Enterprises Limited, 225 Duncan Mill Road, Don Mills, Ontario M3B 3K9, Canada.

This is a work of fiction. Names, characters, places and incidents are either the product of the author's imagination or are used fictitiously, and any resemblance to actual persons, living or dead, business establishments, events or locales is entirely coincidental.

This edition published by arrangement with Harlequin Books S.A.

For questions and comments about the quality of this book, please contact us at CustomerService@Harlequin.com.

® and TM are trademarks of Harlequin Enterprises Limited or its corporate affiliates. Trademarks indicated with ® are registered in the United States Patent and Trademark Office, the Canadian Intellectual Property Office and in other countries.

Printed in U.S.A.

www.Harlequin.com

Chantelle Shaw lives on the Kent coast and thinks up her stories while walking on the beach. She has been married for over thirty years and has six children. Her love affair with reading and writing Harlequin Presents® books began as a teenager, and her first book was published in 2006. She likes strong-willed, slightly unusual characters. Chantelle also loves gardening, walking and wine!

Books by Chantelle Shaw

Harlequin Presents

To Wear His Ring Again
A Night in the Prince's Bed
Captive in His Castle
At Dante's Service
The Greek's Acquisition
Behind the Castello Doors
The Ultimate Risk

The Bond of Brothers

His Unexpected Legacy
Secrets of a Powerful Man

Irresistible Italians

A Dangerous Infatuation

After Hours With The Greek

After the Greek Affair

Visit the Author Profile page
at Harlequin.com for more titles.

For my sister Helen, with love.

CHAPTER ONE

'WHAT LUNATIC DECIDED to go sailing in this atrocious weather?' Lexi muttered into her headset as she piloted the coastguard rescue helicopter over the south coast of England and out across the Solent.

The narrow strait which separated the mainland from the Isle of Wight was a popular area for water sports and on a summer's day, when the sea was calm and blue, it was an idyllic sight to watch the yachts skim across the water with their sails tugging in the breeze. But October had blown in on a series of ferocious storms that had swept away the last remnants of summer and whipped the sea into mountainous waves which crashed against the chalk cliffs, spewing foam high into the air. The white horses reared up in the glare of the helicopter's searchlight but Lexi knew that an even greater threat lay beneath the sea's surface, where dangerous currents eddied and swirled, ready to drag the unwary and unwise down into the depths.

She heard the co-pilot, Gavin's response through her headphones. 'The yacht which has made an emergency call for assistance was competing in a race. Apparently the skipper thought they would be able to run ahead of the storm, but they've hit a sandbank and the boat is taking in water.'

Lexi swore beneath her breath. 'The skipper took a dangerous gamble to win a race. Jeez, I love the male ego!'

'To be fair, the storm is stronger than the Met Office predicted,' Gavin said. 'The complex tidal patterns of the Solent have caught out many experienced sailors.'

'The problem is that too many sailors *don't* have enough experience and fail to appreciate how unpredictable and dangerous the sea can be, like the man on holiday with his son who we were called to assist two days ago. The boy was only ten years old. He didn't stand a chance when their boat started to sink in rough seas.'

'We did all we could,' Gavin reminded her.

'Yeah, but we couldn't save the boy. He was just a kid with his whole life in front of him. What a bloody waste.'

Lexi struggled to bring her emotions under

control and concentrated on flying the helicopter in the strong wind and driving rain. She prided herself on her professionalism. The first rule of working for the rescue service was not to allow your mind to linger on past events—even something as traumatic as the death of a child—but to move on and deal with the next incident.

'The Mayday call confirmed that the three males on the yacht are all wearing life jackets,' Gavin said. 'But they're unlikely to survive for long in these rough seas. The skipper reported that he has received a head injury, but he insisted that he wants his crewmen to be rescued first.'

'It's a bit late for him to be concerned for his crew now. It's a pity he didn't take their safety into account earlier and abort the race.'

Lexi constantly moved her gaze between the flight instrument panel and the window to scan the wild waves below. Three massive chalk stacks known as the Needles rose out of the sea like jagged teeth. The famous landmark was iconic but the strong currents around the rocks could be treacherous.

An orange glow suddenly flashed in the sky. 'Did you see the flare?' Gavin peered through the windscreen as Lexi took the chopper lower. A few moments later he gave another shout. 'I've got a visual—on your right-hand side.'

Lexi spotted the yacht. It had been tipped onto its side by the strong sea swell, and she could make out three figures clinging onto the rigging. She kept the helicopter hovering in position as Gavin went to the rear of the aircraft and prepared to lower the winchman, who was a paramedic, onto the stricken vessel. The buffeting wind made Lexi's job almost impossible, but she was a highly experienced pilot and had flown Chinook helicopters over the deserts of Afghanistan. A cool head and nerves of steel had been necessary when she had been a member of the RAF and those qualities were required for her job with the coastguard rescue agency.

She spoke to the paramedic over the radio. 'Chris, once you're aboard the vessel, remind the crew that the coastguard agency are in charge of the rescue and everyone is to follow your orders, including the skipper. If his head injury looks serious we'll winch him up first, whether he likes it or not. This is not the time for him to decide he wants to be a hero,' she said sardonically.

CHAPTER TWO

THE SEARING PAIN that felt as though Kadir's skull had been split open with an axe was the result of being hit on the head by the sail boom of the *White Hawk*—his brand-new racing yacht that was now residing at the bottom of the sea. However, his immediate concern was not for the loss of his boat but the welfare of his crew, who were being stretchered off the helicopter that had just landed at a hospital on the mainland.

The rescue had been dramatic—and just in time. Once Kadir had realised the yacht was sinking, everything had happened so quickly. He hadn't had time to feel fear, but for a few seconds he had pictured himself galloping across a golden desert on his black stallion Baha', and his heart had ached for what would become of the kingdom his father had entrusted to him.

But, like a miracle, out of the dark sky had appeared a shining light, and he had heard the distinctive *whump-whump* of helicopter rotor blades. Kadir had flown in a helicopter many times, and as he'd clung to the rigging of his wrecked yacht being battered by forty-foot waves he had recognised the skill and bravery of the pilot flying the coastguard rescue chopper in the worsening gale.

He knew that he and his crew had been lucky to survive. But the two young sailors who had crewed for him since the start of the race in the Canary Islands were suffering from hypothermia and were in a bad way. As Kadir watched them being wheeled across the helipad, frustration surged through him. His clothes were wet and stiff with sea salt and the wind whipping across the helipad chilled him to his bones. He lifted a hand to his throbbing head and felt a swelling the size of an egg on his temple.

The coastguard paramedic gave him a worried look. 'Sir, please lie down on the stretcher and one of the medical staff will take you down to the A&E department so that your injuries can be treated.'

'I'm fine; I can walk,' Kadir said impatiently. 'It's my crew who I'm concerned about. I wish you had followed my instructions and rescued them first. They got too cold because they were in the sea for so long. You should have winched them up onto the helicopter before you rescued me.'

'I was under instructions to rescue injured casualties first and it was obvious that you had sustained a possibly serious head injury,' the paramedic explained.

'My crew were my responsibility,' Kadir argued. He was interrupted by another voice.

'I hardly think you are in a position to question the professional judgement of a member of the coastguard team when it was *your* poor judgement in deciding to sail in atrocious weather that put your crew in danger.'

Frowning, Kadir turned towards the person who had jumped down from the helicopter cockpit. Like the other members of the rescue team, the figure was wearing a bulky jumpsuit, but as they removed their flight helmet Kadir's confusion grew.

'Who are you?' he demanded.

'Flight Captain Lexi Howard. I was in charge of the rescue operation. The helicopter crew acted under my instructions, which were to winch up injured casualties first.'

'You're...*a woman*!'

The instant the words left his lips Kadir realised he had made a crass fool of himself. There was a crowd of people standing on the helipad—medical staff and a team of firemen, who were required to be present whenever a helicopter landed at the hospital, and everyone fell silent and stared at him.

He could blame his shocked reaction to the female helicopter pilot on his recent trauma of nearly drowning, and also on the fact that—despite the new laws and policy changes he was gradually trying to introduce—gender equality was still a relatively new concept in his country, the isolated desert kingdom of Zenhab. But it was obvious from the pilot's icy expression that any excuse Kadir might offer for his tactless comment would not be well received.

'Full marks for observation,' the Flight Captain said drily. 'If the fact that I'm a woman bothers you so much I could always drop you back in the sea where I found you and your crew.'

The reminder of the two injured sailors reignited Kadir's sense of frustration that he was not in charge of the situation. He was used to making decisions and having them obeyed without question, and he was struggling to accept that in this instance the female Flight Captain was in control. It didn't help matters that his head felt as if it was going to explode. He gritted his teeth, fighting the nausea that threatened to overwhelm him and destroy what was left of his dignity.

'As the yacht's skipper, it was my duty to ensure the safety of my crew,' he insisted. 'I was in a better position to judge their physical condition than you were and I could see that they were both exhausted.'

'It was my duty to ensure the safety of *all* the casualties in need of rescue, as well as the safety of my flight crew,' the Flight Captain said coldly. 'How dare you question my authority?'

How dare he? No one had ever dared to address Kadir with such insolence, least of all a woman, and certainly not in public. The knowledge that he was indebted to this self-assured young woman for saving his life made him feel emasculated. The fact that she was the most beautiful woman he had ever seen only made him feel worse.

In the nightclubs and casinos—the playgrounds across Europe of the rich and bored—Kadir had met countless beautiful women, and in his youth he had bedded more of them than he cared to remember. For the past decade he had lived his life in the fast lane and played hard, but at thirty-two he felt jaded. It was a long time since his curiosity had been aroused by a woman, but Flight Captain Lexi Howard intrigued him.

Beneath the floodlights on the helipad, her

complexion was flawless and so fair that the skin stretched over her high, slanting cheekbones was almost translucent. Her long braid of ash-blonde hair suggested possible Nordic ancestry and the impression was further enhanced by her light blue eyes that reminded Kadir of the cool, clear skies above the Swiss Alps where he skied every winter.

He found he could not look away from her and he felt a sudden tightness in his chest as if a fist had gripped his heart. Heat surged through his veins. He tried to convince himself that the fire inside him was a natural response after his recent brush with death, but deep in his core something hot and hungry stirred.

'Surely you checked the Met Office shipping forecast and realised that a storm was approaching?' Lexi glared at the yacht's skipper, infuriated that he'd had the cheek to criticise how the rescue operation had been carried out. She guessed he was an inexperienced sailor, and his failure to respond to the worsening weather conditions had compromised the safety of his crew.

Her mind flew back to the incident the coastguard helicopter had attended two days ago and the young boy they had been unable to save. 'Not every rescue can be successful,' the coastguard station commander had reminded

Lexi at the debriefing afterwards. 'Part of the job is to accept that you can't save everyone.'

Lexi's RAF commanding officer of the Medical Emergency Rescue Team in Afghanistan had said the same thing. Many of the things she had seen, the terrible injuries received by soldiers caught in landmine explosions and sniper fire, had been harrowing, but if she had gone to pieces she wouldn't have been able to do her job. The same was true working for the coastguard rescue. Her common sense told her she must not allow one tragedy to haunt her, but in her heart she had taken the failure to save the boy hard.

The tragedy two days ago and the incident today could have been avoided if the yacht's skipper in each case had acted more responsibly, she thought grimly. She was tempted to tell the man standing in front of her what she thought of him, but something about him made her swallow her angry words. Despite his dishevelled appearance and the large purple swelling above his right eye, he had an aura of power about him that set him apart from other men.

He was looking at Lexi in a way that no man had looked at her for a long time. *Too long*— the treacherous thought slid into her head. She tried to push it away but a picture flashed into her mind of the man's strong, tanned hands on her body, dark against pale, hard muscle pressed against soft yielding flesh.

Shocked by her wayward imagination, she narrowed her eyes to hide her thoughts as she studied him. He was sinfully attractive, with exotic olive-gold skin and over-long, thick black hair that curled at his nape and fell forward onto his brow so that he raked it back with an impatient flick of his hand. Lexi's gaze was drawn to his dark brown eyes—liquid pools of chocolate fringed by ridiculously long, silky lashes and set beneath heavy black brows. The gleam in his eyes unsettled her, and the blatantly sensual curve of his lips made her wonder how it would feel if he pressed his mouth against hers.

She shook her head, trying to break free from the disturbing effect he had on her, praying he hadn't noticed that she had been staring at him. She did not understand her reaction to him. It had been a long time since she had looked at a man and felt a quiver in her belly. Too long, she acknowledged ruefully.

'You should have waited for the weather to improve, instead of putting your life and the lives of your crew at risk.' She spoke sharply, desperate to hide her confusing awareness of the yacht's skipper. 'Your behaviour was irresponsible. Offshore sailing is not for inexperienced sailors.'

The man arrogantly threw back his head, drawing Lexi's attention to his broad shoulders. She assessed him to be several inches over six feet tall.

'I'm not a fool,' he said curtly. 'Of course I checked the marine forecast and I was aware of the storm. The *White Hawk* could easily have run ahead of the bad weather, but we must have hit something in the water that ripped the keel from the hull and resulted in the yacht capsizing.'

He broke off abruptly. Following the direction of his gaze, Lexi saw two men hurrying towards them. The helipad was strictly out of bounds to the public but, as she stepped forward to ask the men to leave, they halted in front of the *White Hawk*'s skipper and, to Lexi's astonishment, bowed to him. She had learned enough Arabic during her tours of duty in the Middle East to recognise the language they spoke. After a brief conversation with the men, the skipper swung away from Lexi without giving her another glance and strode across the helipad, followed by his two companions.

'A word of thanks for saving his life would have been nice,' she said disgustedly, not caring if her words carried across the helipad to him. She glanced at the coastguard paramedic. 'Did you see how those men bowed to him as if they were his servants? He actually clicked his fingers for them to follow him! Who the hell does he think he is?'

Chris gave her an amused look. 'I take it from the way you ripped into him that you didn't recognise him? That was His Royal Highness, Sultan Kadir Al Sulaimar of Zenhab, and I'm guessing that the men who came to collect him *are* his servants. Not only is he a Sultan, he was the skipper of the Zenhab Team Valiant who won the America's Cup in the summer.' He grinned at Lexi's startled expression. 'I got the feeling that he didn't take kindly to you calling him an inexperienced sailor.'

'I still think he was irresponsible to have sailed when he knew that a storm was coming,' Lexi argued. 'But I guess he couldn't have known his yacht's keel would fail,' she conceded reluctantly. She knew enough about sailing to be aware that catastrophic keel failure was uncommon but not unheard of, and it was the main cause of yachts capsizing quickly, giving the crew little warning or time to radio for assistance.

She winced as she remembered how she had accused the man of being an inexperienced sailor. Now that she thought about it, he *had* seemed vaguely familiar, she mused as she climbed into the helicopter cockpit and prepared to take off from the helipad. During the summer there had been extensive news coverage of the famous America's Cup yacht race held in San Francisco, when the Zenhabian Team Valiant had beaten Team USA to win the prestigious trophy. Sultan Kadir Al Sulaimar had been interviewed on live television by an overexcited female presenter who had clearly been overwhelmed by his exotic looks and undeniable charm.

Lexi told herself that it wasn't surprising that she had failed to recognise the Sultan when he had been battered, bruised and dripping wet after being rescued from his sinking yacht. To her annoyance, she could not stop thinking about him. At the end of her shift she went back to the old coastguard cottage that had been her home for the past year but, instead of finishing packing up her belongings ready to move out, she wasted an hour looking up Sultan Kadir Al Sulaimar on her laptop.

She had no trouble finding pictures of him, mostly taken at social events in Europe. He was invariably accompanied by a beautiful woman. Blonde, brunette or redhead, it seemed that the Sultan had no particular preference but, from the dizzying number of different women he was photographed with, it appeared that he liked variety. According to the press reports, he was a playboy with a personal fortune estimated to be in the billions. He owned a luxury chalet in St Moritz, penthouses in New York and London's Mayfair and an English country estate where he kept racehorses.

There was some information about the country he ruled. Zenhab was an independent Arab kingdom in the Arabian Sea. Kadir had succeeded his father, Sultan Khalif Al Sulaimar, who was credited with establishing peace in Zenhab after years of fighting between rival tribal groups. But while the previous Sultan had rarely travelled abroad or courted the attention of the world's media, his son was frequently spotted by the paparazzi at nightclubs in Paris, or at Ascot, where he owned a private box and entertained celebrities and members of the British royal family, or driving his attention-grabbing scarlet sports car around Belgravia.

In short, the spoiled Sultan was the absolute antithesis of the kind of man Lexi admired. When she had served in Afghanistan, she had met men who were brave and loyal and utterly dedicated to carrying out the missions they had been assigned even though their lives were often at risk.

The memory of how the Sultan had looked at her with a predatory gleam in his eyes slid into her mind and her stomach muscles clenched. Sexual attraction followed its own rules and ignored common sense, she thought ruefully. Or maybe it was just her body reminding her that it was perfectly normal for a twenty-nine-year-old woman to feel sexual desire.

It was over a year since she had broken up with Steven—or, to be more precise, since he'd informed her in a text message hours before their engagement party that he couldn't marry her because he had a girlfriend and a baby daughter who he had failed to mention when he and Lexi had grown close while they had been stationed together at Camp Bastion. Rejection hurt as much at twenty-eight as it had when she had been eighteen or eight, Lexi had discovered. She had dealt with Steven's betrayal the same way she had dealt with all the disappointments in her life, by pretending that she did not give a damn and hiding her feelings from a world that had proved too often that people were unreliable.

Perhaps the women in the newspaper photographs, clinging like limpets to the Sultan of Zenhab, had the right idea, she brooded.

At least if you were a playboy's mistress you would have no expectations that he might commit to the relationship or fall in love with you. And no doubt the sex was amazing!

As Lexi visualised Sultan Kadir Al Sulaimar's arrogantly handsome face, heat unfurled in the pit of her stomach. She would never be tempted to sacrifice her hard-won pride and self-respect for five minutes in the sexy Sultan's bed, she assured herself. An hour on the treadmill followed by a brisk shower left her physically spent, but when she flopped into bed she was kept awake by the memory of the sensual promise in his molten chocolate eyes.

Two days later, Lexi donned her coastguard agency uniform for the last time, checked the gold buttons on her jacket were gleaming and adjusted her cap, before she walked into the station commander's office.

'I'm sorry to lose you,' Roger Norris told her. 'You've done a fantastic job over the past year.'

'I'm sorry to go,' Lexi said honestly. 'I'm going to miss everyone on the team, but I knew when I came here that the contract for a second helicopter pilot was only for one year.'

'The number of rescues you have carried out has proved the need for a second rescue helicopter, but unfortunately the funding for the coastguard agency has been cut.' Roger's frown cleared. 'However, I have received a piece of good news. A private donor has offered to pay for a permanent second helicopter and crew. The details will still have to be ironed out over the next few months but, if the offer goes ahead, would you be interested in resuming your role of Flight Captain?'

Lexi's eyebrows rose. 'I'd certainly consider it. Whoever the private donor is must be very wealthy.'

'He's a billionaire, by all accounts. You met him two nights ago—' Roger chuckled '—although I heard from Gavin and Chris that you didn't recognise him. In fact you're the reason that Sultan Kadir of Zenhab has made his incredibly generous offer after you rescued him and his crewmen from his capsized yacht. He has asked to see you so that he can thank you personally. He's staying in the Queen Mary suite at the Admiralty Hotel and requested for you to meet him there at six o'clock this evening.'

Lexi's heart collided painfully with her ribs at the mention of the Sultan. She flushed as she recalled the shockingly erotic dreams she'd had about him for the past two nights. She was behaving like a schoolgirl with a crush on a member of a boy band, she thought disgustedly.

'I'm afraid it won't be possible for me to meet him,' she told Roger. 'I'm going to my sister's engagement party this evening and it's a couple of hours' drive to Henley, where Athena's fiancé's parents live. Can't Chris or Gavin go instead of me?'

Roger shook his head. 'Chris is on duty. Gavin is at the hospital with Kate, and it looks as though her labour pains aren't a false alarm this time. Anyway, the Sultan particularly asked to see you.

'I'll be honest, Lexi. It is vital that the coastguard agency secures his donation. This part of the south coast is a busy area for shipping, and the rescue service needs a second helicopter. Perhaps you could phone the hotel and arrange to meet His Highness this afternoon instead of this evening?' Roger gave her a level look. 'It might also be a good idea to apologise to him. I understand that you had a heated exchange of words with him the other night.'

Lexi frowned at the reminder that she had behaved less than professionally when she had argued with the skipper of the capsized yacht, unaware that he was the Sultan of Zenhab and an experienced sailor. But the coastguard commander's words tugged on her conscience. The

Sultan's offer to make permanent funds available for a second helicopter was astonishingly generous and could mean the difference between life and death for accident victims on the south coast who needed to be urgently transferred to hospital.

She stood up. 'I suppose I could stop off at the Admiralty Hotel and meet him before I drive to the party,' she said reluctantly.

'Good. And Lexi, be nice to him.'

She turned in the doorway and gave Roger a puzzled look. 'I'm always nice, aren't I?'

'Certainly—' the commander smiled |'—but you can be intimidating. You have an outstanding war record and demonstrated your exceptional bravery, both in the RAF and as a civilian rescue pilot. Sometimes people, men especially, are in awe of you.'

Lexi visualised the Sultan of Zenhab's haughty features and gave a snort. She couldn't imagine His High and Mightiness had ever felt intimidated.

Driving back to the cottage, Roger's comment played on her mind. Did people really find her intimidating? She had always been a popular member of her RAF squadron and, since coming to work for the coastguard agency, she had quickly established her place in the team. The guys treated her as one of them, yet she sensed a faint reservation in their attitude. She had thought it was because she was the only female rescue pilot. But it had been the same when she had been at boarding school. She'd got on well with the other girls but she had never made close friendships.

She telephoned the Admiralty Hotel, and when a vague-sounding receptionist told her that the Sultan was unavailable to take her call she left a message explaining that she could meet him at five o'clock rather than six.

The rest of the day was spent packing up her car with bags and boxes. Closing the door of the cottage for the last time, she felt an unexpected pang. After ten years in the RAF, constantly moving to wherever in the world her squadron was deployed, she had enjoyed making the cottage into a home—even though it had not been the home she had imagined she would share with Steven.

He had talked about them buying a house together. They had even visited an estate agent to discuss the kind of property they wanted, Lexi remembered. Just for a while she had bought into the daydream of a happy marriage, children—a family that was truly her own and a sense of belonging, after a lifetime of feeling that she did not belong anywhere. She should have guessed it was too good to be true. Steven's betrayal had reminded her of the sense of rejection she had felt when her parents had made it obvious that they preferred their own daughter, Athena, who had been born to them a year after they had adopted Lexi.

At five minutes to five, Lexi walked across the foyer of the Admiralty Hotel, praying that she would not slip in her stiletto heels on the polished marble floor. Usually she lived in jeans and running trainers, but because she was on a tight schedule she had changed into a black silk jersey dress that was suitable for a cocktail party and wouldn't crease while she was sitting in the car.

The hotel receptionist looked flustered as she dealt with a coach party of tourists who had just arrived. Lexi checked in the lounge and bar, but there was no sign of the Sultan. She glanced at her watch and decided she would have to take charge of the situation. Abandoning the idea of trying to catch the receptionist's attention, she walked over to the lift and asked a porter for directions to the Queen Mary suite.

CHAPTER THREE

KADIR WALKED INTO his hotel suite and took a moment to appreciate the rare luxury of being completely alone. At the royal palace in Zenhab he was always surrounded by courtiers and government ministers, and a retinue of staff and security personnel accompanied him when he visited his various homes in Europe. Even while he had been staying here in a tiny village on the south coast of England he'd given in to pressure from his chief adviser and brought two security guards with him, as well as his private secretary and his manservant Walif, who, despite his seventy-one years, insisted on serving the Sultan as he had served Kadir's father.

Since his yachting accident two days ago, his staff had driven him mad with their concern for his well-being and, fond as he was of Walif, he had struggled to control his irritation when the manservant had flapped around him like a mother hen. Earlier today, Kadir's patience had finally snapped and he had sent everyone to his house in Windsor to wait for him.

The sense of freedom reminded him of how he felt when he raced his stallion Baha' across the desert with the cool wind whipping his face and a million stars studding the purple sky. Free from Walif's anxious concern for his health, he had spent two hours working out in the hotel gym.

The swelling above his eyebrow had almost disappeared, he noted, glancing in the bathroom mirror before he stepped into the shower cubicle. He had been lucky that the blow to his head from the sail boom had not knocked him unconscious, and even luckier that he had escaped from the capsized yacht with his life. Although it had not been luck, but the skill and bravery of the coastguard rescue crew, and especially the Flight Captain who had flown the helicopter in atrocious weather conditions.

Kadir pictured Lexi Howard's face. Her delicate features—the finely arched brows, defined cheekbones and perfect Cupid's bow lips—reminded him of the exquisite porcelain figurines in his grandmother's collection, which were displayed in a glass cabinet at Montgomery Manor. But the Flight Captain's fragile appearance was deceptive. He frowned, remembering her sharp voice and the dismissive way she had flicked her frosty blue eyes over him.

Immediately after he had been rescued from his doomed yacht, Kadir's pride had stung worse than his cracked skull. But now, with his equilibrium restored, he found Ms Howard's attitude refreshing. It had been a novelty to meet a woman who did not fawn on him or flirt with him. Too often he had found it too easy to persuade women into his bed. When he had been younger he had enjoyed being spoiled for choice, but a life without challenge was boring.

Lexi Howard was definitely a challenge. Desire kicked in Kadir's groin as he thought of the cool blonde beauty. He imagined teasing her mouth open with his tongue and tasting her. How long would it take to break through her reserve until she responded to him? he wondered, picturing her creamy complexion suffused with the rosy flush of sexual arousal.

Closing his eyes, he leaned back against the shower wall and visualised the icy, uptight Flight Captain melting beneath his hands. Slowly, he slid his hand down his body and stretched his fingers around his erection. He pictured Lexi Howard's capable hands on him, caressing him, stroking him lightly and then not so lightly…gripping him hard…

With a groan, he gave in to temptation and the urgent demands of his arousal. The cords in his neck stood out as he tipped his head back and the fire inside him became a furnace. His release came swiftly, awarding him momentary satisfaction that felt somehow incomplete.

But pleasuring himself was his only option, after the decision he had taken six months ago when his future bride had turned twenty-one and under Zenhabian law had become of marriageable age. Out of respect for Haleema, Kadir had ended his affairs with his European mistresses.

In the ten years that he had been Sultan of Zenhab he had been careful to avoid personal scandal in his desert kingdom, and had earned the support and respect of the population. It had been suggested to him by some of his advisers that monogamy was not a requirement of his arranged marriage as long as he was discreet, but he had every intention of fulfilling his role of husband to the best of his ability, to honour the promise he had made to his father.

Kadir had only been sixteen when Sultan Khalif had suffered a stroke that had left him a prisoner in his body—unable to walk, and with limited speech. Under Zenhabian law, the Sultan's brother had been made an interim ruler until the rightful heir came of age. But when Kadir had turned twenty-one, Jamal had been reluctant to hand over the Crown to his nephew, and he'd had support from tribal leaders in the mountain territories.

In order to claim the Crown from his uncle, Kadir had been forced to agree to marry the daughter of Jamal's strongest ally, Sheikh Rashid bin Al-Hassan. At the time he had signed the agreement, Haleema had been a child of eleven. But now she was twenty-one and, since the death of Sheikh Rashid two months ago, Kadir had come under increasing pressure from his uncle to set a date for his wedding. He knew he could not put if off for much longer. Haleema's family would consider a lengthy delay to be an insult to the princess of the mountain tribes, and Jamal—the most poisonous snake in Zenhab—would waste no time stirring up trouble that could threaten the stability of the country.

For the sake of Zenhab and for the love he felt for his father, Kadir would honour his duty. But there was a part of him that rebelled against the old ways of his kingdom. He had been educated in England and at university he had felt envious of his peers, who were free to live their lives without the burden of responsibility that had always been his destiny.

He had never even seen his future bride,

but that would soon change. On his return to Zenhab he would travel to the mountains to meet Haleema's brother Omar, the new leader of the northern tribes, and begin formal proceedings for his marriage. He might even be permitted to meet Haleema, but according to the old customs he would not have an opportunity to be alone with her until she became his wife.

Kadir's thoughts turned once again to Flight Captain Lexi Howard. She had proved when she had rescued him and his crew that she was a highly skilled pilot, hence his decision to offer her a job as his private pilot in Zenhab. He knew it might be viewed as controversial to appoint a woman in what was considered by traditionalists to be a male role, but he fervently believed that his kingdom needed to modernise and accept that women were equal to men. The helicopter he had recently purchased would allow him to travel to Haleema's home in the mountainous northern territories more easily. And with that last thought of Haleema, his future had been decided for him ten years ago, he felt a sense that prison bars were closing around him.

Abruptly he switched off the shower, dried himself and pulled on a pair of trousers. Midway through shaving, he heard a knock on the door of the suite, which he ignored, forgetting that he had sent his staff away. Three impatient raps followed, and he cursed as the razor slipped in his hand and the blade nicked his chin. Grabbing a towel, he strode out of the bathroom and across the sitting room to fling open the door.

'Ms Howard! This is a surprise!'

Lexi frowned. 'Is it? I left a message with reception saying that I would be here at five.'

Kadir recalled that the phone had rung as he'd been on his way out of the door to go to the gym, but he hadn't bothered to answer it. 'I'm afraid I didn't receive any message,' he murmured.

How could his smile be so wickedly sexy? Lexi jerked her eyes from the sensual curve of his mouth and tried to ignore the fact that Sultan Kadir Al Sulaimar was half naked and had obviously just taken a shower. Droplets of water clung to the whorls of black hairs that grew thickly on his chest.

When she had rescued him, his body had been hidden beneath a bulky waterproof sailing suit. But now Lexi was faced with rippling muscles, gleaming olive-gold skin, broad, satin-smooth shoulders and his tight-as-a-drum abdomen.

Her eyes were drawn to the fuzz of black

hairs that arrowed down from his navel and disappeared beneath the waistband of his trousers, which sat low on his hips. Her mouth suddenly felt dry. She lifted her gaze back to his face and her stomach swooped when she discovered that he was even more gorgeous than she remembered from their first meeting.

The combination of his lean, chiselled features and deep-set dark eyes was mesmerising. His mouth was full-lipped, and curved into a sultry smile that sent a tingle through Lexi's body. Her breath seemed to be trapped somewhere between her lungs and her throat. She needed to say something, anything to break the prickling silence that became more intense with every passing second so that she was sure he must be able to hear the loud thud of her heart.

She said the first thing that came into her head. 'You're bleeding…on your chin. No, closer to your lip…' She pointed, trying to direct him as he lifted the towel he was holding and pressed it against his face.

'I started shaving when I was fourteen. You'd think I'd be better at it by now,' he said ruefully. He thrust the towel at her. 'Will you play nurse?'

His voice was as sexy as his smile—deep and rich, caressing her senses and conjuring up images in her mind that were shockingly inappropriate.

'I should go,' she muttered. 'This is obviously not a convenient time...' Not when her heart was beating painfully fast. Lexi did not understand why he affected her so strongly. For ten years she had worked in a predominantly male environment and had met her fair share of good-looking men. *But none like him*, whispered a voice inside her head. Even his title—Sultan of Zenhab—was exotic and made her think of a desert oasis beneath a starry sky, a tent draped with silks, and him, naked, his bronzed, muscular body sprawled on satin cushions and his dark eyes gleaming as he beckoned to her to come to him.

Lexi swallowed. What on *earth* was the matter with her? She felt as though her body was on fire.

'You're not bothered by the sight of blood, are you?'

The amusement in his voice pulled her back from her erotic fantasy. Thank goodness he couldn't possibly have known what she had been thinking. His question jolted her mind back to her experiences of a real desert—the dry, unforgiving landscape, clouds of choking sand stirred up by the downdraught of the Chinook's rotor blades, the screams of wounded men, the smell of blood and dust and vomit.

'No, blood doesn't worry me,' she told him calmly, in control once more. The cut near to his bottom lip was still bleeding. She pressed the corner of the towel against his face and somehow, without her being aware that either of them had moved, she found herself inside his suite and he shut the door.

She immediately became conscious of how close they were standing. His warm breath whispered across her cheek and the mingled scents of soap, his spicy cologne and something more subtle—the sensual musk of maleness—stirred her senses. Her breasts brushed against his bare chest and the contact with his body sent a ripple of awareness through her.

Panic was an unfamiliar emotion for Lexi, but she was shaken by her reaction to the Sultan. She lifted the towel to see if the cut had stopped bleeding and saw that her hand was trembling. In Afghanistan, when she had flown behind enemy lines to pick up casualties, her nerves had been as steady as her hands on the helicopter's control stick. Why did this pampered playboy prince who had probably never done a day's work in his life disturb her?

Thankfully, the cut on his chin had closed up. She handed him the towel and stepped back from him. 'You'll live. I'm sure legions of women will be relieved,' she said drily.

His smile remained fixed, but Lexi sensed a sudden stillness in him that made her think of a panther about to pounce on its hapless prey. She reminded herself that the playboy was also a powerful Sultan who had kept peace in Zenhab despite the often volatile situation in other parts of the Middle East.

'Your sailing accident was widely reported in the press, Your Highness,' she murmured. In fact the tabloids had only carried a paragraph or two about his capsized yacht and had been more interested in reporting stories of his affairs with supermodels and actresses.

It wasn't as if she was in the least bit interested in a promiscuous womaniser, Lexi thought. She had only agreed to meet the Sultan because Roger Norris had asked her to.

'I understand that your yacht has been retrieved from where it sank in the Solent and it was discovered that the keel had been ripped from the hull.' She hesitated. 'I'm afraid I was rather hasty the other night when I jumped to the conclusion that you had ignored the reports of an approaching storm. I…apologise if my attitude was less than professional.'

Kadir just managed to stop himself from laughing out loud at Lexi Howard's grudging apology. She had spoken politely, but he sensed her reluctance to be here. It was obvious that she had been sent to see him, and it was easy to guess the real reason for her visit. Her next words confirmed his suspicion.

'Roger Norris explained that you have made a very generous offer to finance a second rescue helicopter.'

Kadir idly wondered if the coastguard commander had told Lexi to dress up for their meeting and perhaps try to persuade him to donate even more funds. Catching the cool expression in her eyes, he dismissed the idea. No one would dare tell Lexi Howard what to do—which made her choice of outfit interesting.

He ran his eyes over her, noting how the stretchy fabric of her dress moulded her toned figure and emphasised the shape of her firm breasts. The dress stopped at mid-thigh-level and below the hemline her slender legs, sheathed in sheer black hose, looked even longer with the addition of three-inch stiletto heels. Recalling his erotic fantasies about her while he'd been in the shower, Kadir felt the simmering heat in his gut burn hotter.

'The least I can do is to make a contribution to the rescue agency responsible for saving my life and the lives of my crew,' he said abruptly. 'I must also apologise, Captain Howard, for not thanking you for your skill and bravery after the rescue the other night. I am conscious that I owe you a huge debt of gratitude.'

'I was simply doing my job,' she muttered.

'I understand from Roger Norris that you no longer work for the coastguard agency.'

'My contract was only for a year. Although, if there is to be a second rescue helicopter, I might get my job back.'

'But you don't have another job to go to at the moment?' Kadir knew he was staring at Lexi but he could not help himself. She was so damned beautiful! He cleared his throat. 'I asked you to meet me because I have a proposition I want to discuss with you.'

'What kind of proposition?' The gleam of sexual interest in his eyes, and memories of the stories in the newspapers about his playboy lifestyle, sent Lexi's imagination into overdrive.

Kadir was irritated that Lexi obviously believed the garbage which had been written about him in the tabloids. But she was not nearly as composed as she would like him to think. Her breathing was shallow and the downwards sweep of her long eyelashes was too late to hide her dilated pupils. He roamed his eyes over her in a slow, deliberate appraisal, and was rewarded when the hard points of her nipples became clearly discernible beneath her clingy dress.

Suddenly he understood, and a feeling of satisfaction swept through him. He had seen her scornful expression when she'd referred to the reports of his alleged playboy lifestyle. Most of the stories about his private life, which had been printed alongside the news of his yachting accident, were either rehashed from years ago or greatly exaggerated. Kadir had felt no inclination to defend himself to Lexi, but he'd been annoyed by her readiness to judge him.

Now, as he watched her cross her arms defensively over her breasts, he realised that the waves of antagonism she had been sending out were a frantic attempt to disguise the fact that she was attracted to him. Perhaps she hoped that her frosty attitude disguised her sexual awareness of him, but Kadir *knew*—just as he always knew when a woman was interested in him. He had played the game of chasing women who wanted to be caught too often, he thought cynically.

But this time the rules were different. When he returned to Zenhab he would honour the promise he had made to his father and marry the bride who had been chosen for him. Although he desired the Flight Captain, he had no intention of actually catching her. But Lexi did not know that!

'Why don't we sit down,' he murmured, 'and make ourselves comfortable?'

Lexi swallowed as she watched the Sultan lower himself onto the sofa. He stretched his arms along the back, drawing her attention to his bare torso. His broad shoulders gleamed like burnished copper in the golden autumn sunshine slanting through the window, and his chest and forearms were covered in a fine mat of silky black hairs that accentuated his raw masculinity.

Conscious that her heart was thudding uncomfortably fast, she made a show of checking her watch. 'I really must be going. I expect you want to finish getting dressed,' she said pointedly, 'and I have to be somewhere at seven-thirty, and I want to hit the motorway before the evening traffic builds up.'

'Do you have a date this evening? And there I was thinking you had worn that very sexy dress especially to meet me,' Kadir drawled.

Lexi flushed. 'It is not a sexy dress,' she said tightly. 'It's a cocktail dress suitable for a cocktail party to celebrate my sister's engagement.' The idea that the Sultan assumed she'd dressed up for him was infuriating but, to her shame, she felt a frisson of awareness shoot through her when his dark eyes gleamed with a hard brilliance.

'Surely you don't have to leave just yet if the party doesn't start for another two hours?' To Lexi's consternation, he sprang up from the sofa and walked over to her, moving with the speed and grace of a jungle cat. He was too close and towered over her so that she had to tilt her head to meet his intent gaze. Heat radiated from his body, or maybe the heat came from her, making her feel flushed and flustered and acutely aware of her femininity.

Desperate to hide the effect he had on her, she launched into an explanation. 'The journey to Henley-on-Thames, which is where my sister's fiancé's parents live, will take over an hour, and I daren't risk being late and upsetting Lady Fairfax.'

Lexi frowned as she recalled how tense her sister had sounded on the phone. Athena had confided her worry that Charles's parents did not approve of their son's choice of bride because they had hoped he would marry someone with a similar aristocratic pedigree to the Fairfaxes. 'The engagement party is my chance to prove that I can be a good wife to Charlie and a sophisticated hostess when he invites business clients to dinner,' Athena had said earnestly.

Lexi had struggled to picture her accident-prone sister as a sophisticated hostess, but she had kept her doubts that Charles Fairfax was the right man for Athena to herself.

Her thoughts scattered when Sultan Kadir spoke. His deep, dark voice curled around her like a lover's caress. She caught her breath as he lifted his hand and brushed the back of his knuckles oh-so-lightly down her cheek. It was a blatant invasion of her personal space but her feet seemed to be rooted to the floor and she could not step away from him.

'I am disappointed that you must rush away before we've had a chance to discuss my proposal. Perhaps we can arrange to meet again at a more convenient time?'

She licked her dry lips and told herself she was imagining the predatory gleam in his eyes. 'Your Highness…' Her voice sounded strangely breathless.

'Please call me Kadir, Lexi.'

The way he said her name, with that soft huskiness in his voice, was too intimate, as if he had stroked each syllable with his tongue.

Lexi felt as though she was drowning in his molten gaze, but a tiny part of her sanity remained and asked why she was letting him get to her. He was a notorious womaniser, and in the past when other men like him had tried to come on to her she'd had no trouble shooting them down.

Of course she would not allow herself to be seduced by the Sultan, she assured herself. But she could not deny that his interest was flattering and a salve to her wounded pride after Steven's betrayal. Without conscious thought, she swayed towards Kadir, bringing her mouth even closer to his. Her heart pounded and her eyelashes swept down as she waited, tense with anticipation, for him to brush his lips over hers.

'You've been a long time in the shower. I've been getting bored waiting for you.'

Lexi froze and jerked her head towards the petulant female voice. Shock slithered like an ice cube down her spine when she saw a woman standing in the doorway that connected the sitting room and bedroom. Through the open door she could see a big bed with rumpled sheets. The woman—girl—was no more than seventeen. Lexi recognised she was Tania Stewart, daughter of the local yacht club president Derek Stewart, who also owned the Admiralty Hotel.

Tania frowned at Lexi. 'What are you doing here?' She turned her wide-eyed gaze to the Sultan and allowed the sheet that was draped around her body to slip down, revealing her bare breasts. 'Don't keep me waiting any longer, Kadir,' she murmured in a sex kitten voice that somehow emphasised how painfully young she was.

'Go and put some clothes on, Tania.' In contrast, Kadir spoke in a clipped tone that was as coldly regal as his expression, Lexi noted, when she looked at him.

She instantly grasped the situation—it didn't take a genius to work out what was going on—and she felt sick at her stupidity. How could she have almost been taken in by the playboy prince's charisma? It stung her pride to realise that she had no more sense than the silly girl who had just crawled out of his bed.

She glanced at Tania and back to Kadir. The reason he was half undressed in the afternoon was now abundantly clear and she supposed she should be thankful that he had pulled on a pair of trousers before he'd opened the door to her.

'Forgive me, Your Highness, for not staying around to discuss your proposition, but I'm not into threesomes,' she said, her voice as biting as a nuclear winter.

His only response was to lift his eyebrows as if he found her reaction amusing.

Lexi's temper simmered. She looked at Tania, who had at least draped the sheet more strategically around her naked body, and back at Kadir. 'You bastard. She's just a kid. Is that how you get your kicks?'

His eyes glittered with anger, but Lexi did not give him a chance to speak. She despised him, and at that moment she despised herself for her weakness. Dear heaven, she had actually wanted him to kiss her! Even now, as she wheeled away from him and marched across the room, her legs trembled and she had to fight the urge to turn her head and look at him one last time, to imprint his outrageously gorgeous facial features on her mind. Pride prevailed and she walked out of the door, closing it with a decisive snap behind her.

CHAPTER FOUR

KADIR WATCHED LEXI HOWARD across the ballroom and felt a slow burn of desire in the pit of his stomach. She was startlingly beautiful, and he noticed that many of the other party guests glanced at her more than once. There was something almost ethereal about her ash-blonde hair, swept up into a chignon tonight, and her peaches and cream complexion. Her fine bone structure, with those high cheekbones, was simply exquisite. She was an English rose, combining cool elegance with understated sensuality in her short black dress and her endlessly long legs and high-heeled black shoes.

If he was a betting man he would lay money that she was wearing stockings. Kadir's nostrils flared as he visualised her wrapping her legs around his back, wearing the stockings and stilettos—and nothing else!

He frowned and altered his position in an effort to ease the hard throb of his arousal. It was a long time since he'd felt so intensely turned on by a woman, especially by a woman who clearly disliked him. In fact it had never happened to him before. Since his youth, women had thrown themselves at him.

Perhaps it was simply the novelty of Lexi Howard's frosty attitude that intrigued him. His mind flew to those few moments in his hotel room when he had nearly kissed her. What had started out as an amusing game had quickly and unexpectedly turned into something darker and hotter when he'd seen the invitation in her eyes.

He wondered what would have happened if the teenager Tania Stewart, who had followed him around like a lovesick puppy while he had been staying at her father's hotel, had not made her spectacular appearance. Kadir knew he would have covered Lexi's mouth with his and tasted her—and she would have let him. Instead, she had treated him like a pariah. His jaw clenched. The scalding fury that had been responsible for him gunning his sports car up the motorway still simmered inside him like the smouldering embers of a fire.

'I see you're looking at my future sister-in-law.'

Kadir's bland expression gave away none

of his thoughts as he turned his head towards the man standing beside him. Charles Fairfax's face had the ruddy hue of a man who was on his fifth gin punch, even though it was still early in the evening. 'I'd better warn you, old man. You won't get any joy there. A couple of my friends have tried and reported that Lexi Howard is a frigid bitch. It's no surprise her fiancé dumped her. The guy was lucky the ice queen didn't freeze his balls off.' Charles laughed, evidently finding his schoolboy attempt at humour funny.

Charles had always been a pain in the backside when they had been at school, Kadir mused, fixing a smile on his lips to disguise his temptation to rearrange Charles's nondescript features with his fist. In truth, he was puzzled by his violent reaction to the Englishman's crude comments, and his desire to defend Lexi Howard. At Eton College he had never considered Charles Fairfax to be a close friend but, thanks to social media, he had remained in touch with many of his fellow students from his school days. Networking was always useful, and when Lexi had mentioned her sister's engagement party Kadir had known that there was only one Lord and Lady Fairfax living in Henley-on-Thames.

His eyes strayed across the room to where

Lexi was chatting to a petite woman with a mass of dark brown hair and wearing a dress in an unflattering shade of acid-yellow. It was curious that the Howard sisters were so unalike, he thought.

He saw Lexi glance around the room and stiffen when she noticed him. From across the ballroom he felt waves of hostility emanating from her, challenging him, exciting him. Kadir felt his heart jolt against his ribs. He held Lexi's gaze as he raised his glass to her, before he sipped his Virgin Mary, feeling the peppery warmth of the drink heat his blood.

'Do you think I look fat in this dress? I wish I could wear black like you but it makes my skin look sallow.'

Lexi forced her mind from the humiliating spectacle that had taken place in Sultan Kadir of Zenhab's hotel suite earlier and concentrated on her sister. 'You look lovely,' she said, in what she hoped was a convincing voice.

Athena's face brightened. 'Lady Fairfax helped me to choose my dress. She said the colour suits me.'

'Did she?' Lexi suspected that Charles Fairfax's mother had her reasons for persuading Athena to wear the ghastly yellow satin dress. Charles was her only son and would eventu-

ally become the next Lord Fairfax, and Lexi
had overheard several party guests comment
that Charles's parents wished him to marry a
woman with a title.

Athena fiddled with the large satin bow on
her shoulder. 'I wish I looked elegant and sophisticated like you,' she blurted. 'You would
be a much better wife for Charlie than me.
You would know how to talk to people at dinner parties, and you'd never spill your wine or
drop your spoon into the soup. I'm so clumsy.
Sometimes I think Charlie finds me an embarrassment.'

Lexi frowned. 'You can't help being short-
sighted. Charlie should be more supportive.
Presumably he asked you to marry him because he loves you, not because he wants you
to be his unpaid social hostess.' She gave her
sister an exasperated look and was tempted
to ask Athena why she had agreed to marry
Charles, who was a wimp with a distinctly
spiteful side to his nature. 'To be honest, I'm
not convinced that he's the right man for you.'

'Maybe you're jealous that I'm getting married and you're not.' Athena bit her lip. 'I'm
sorry, Lexi. That was a horrible thing to say.
It's just that since you broke up with Steven
you've pushed people away more than ever,
including Mum and Dad…and me.'

'I was over Steven a long time ago,' Lexi said curtly. 'I don't push people away.' She remembered the coastguard commander Roger Norris's comment that she came across as intimidating. 'I admit I'm independent, but I had to be when I was growing up. I always knew I had been adopted, but you are Marcus and Veronica's own daughter and it was natural that they doted on you.'

Athena looked as though she was going to cry and Lexi silently cursed her runaway tongue. It wasn't her sister's fault that she had been the favourite child.

'Mum and Dad are really proud of you, and they're always telling people that you were a pilot in the RAF and received an award for bravery for your work in Afghanistan. They wanted to catch up with you tonight, but they couldn't make the party because their cruise was booked ages ago.

'I'm sure Mum and Dad wish I was as clever as you,' Athena admitted. 'They are both doctors and I suppose they naturally assumed I would be academic like them. They even named me after the Greek goddess of wisdom, for heaven's sake! I know they were disappointed when I failed to get the grades to go to university. At least they're pleased that

I'm going to marry Charlie and I'll be Lady Fairfax one day.'

'You can't marry him just to win parental approval.'

'I'm not… Of course I love him,' Athena insisted, too earnestly, in Lexi's opinion. But she did not voice her concerns. Her sister was an adult and perfectly able to decide who she wanted to marry. In truth, Lexi was surprised that Athena had confided in her. The close bond they had shared as children had faded when Lexi had been sent away to boarding school.

She looked around the room. 'Where is Charlie, anyway? This is your engagement party but I haven't seen him all evening.'

'Oh, he's with one of his old school friends from Eton. Charlie was so surprised when Earl Montgomery phoned out of the blue earlier this evening and said he would like to catch up on old times. Naturally, Charlie immediately invited him to the party. I think they must still be in the library.' Athena squinted around the room. 'Oh, look, they're over by the bar. The Earl is very good-looking, don't you think? But don't tell Charlie I said so, will you?' she said worriedly.

Lexi could not reply. She felt as though her breath had been squeezed out of her lungs as she stared across the room and saw Sultan Kadir Al Sulaimar's mouth curl into a mocking smile. What the hell was he doing here at her sister's engagement party, pretending to be a member of the British aristocracy? She frowned. He couldn't be an imposter because Athena had said he had been at Eton with Charlie. But it was too much of a coincidence that the Sultan, or Earl or whatever he was, had decided to call up his old school friend tonight of all nights.

It was impossible not to compare the two men as they approached. Charles, sandy-haired and weak-chinned, was at least five inches shorter than his companion. But it wasn't only Sultan Kadir's height that set him apart from every other man in the room. He was like an exotic bird of paradise among a flock of pigeons, Lexi thought. His olive-gold skin gleamed beneath the sparkling chandeliers, and his hot chocolate eyes were slumberous and sensual, promising wicked delights that turned Lexi's insides to liquid. The last time she'd seen him he had been half-undressed, but he was no less devastating wearing a black dinner suit that had been expertly tailored to sheath his muscular body.

She hid her fierce tension behind a cool smile as Charlie made introductions, but the glint in Sultan Kadir's eyes told her he was aware of her reluctance to shake his hand; he clasped her fingers for a fraction too long and watched with interest the jerky rise and fall of her breasts as she sucked in a breath.

Lexi could not bring herself to allude to their earlier meeting at his hotel. She shuddered at the memory of how she had swayed towards him and practically begged him to kiss her. She wanted to believe that even if Tania had not interrupted them she would have come to her senses before anything had happened, but her pounding heart mocked that idea.

She affected a puzzled expression. 'I'm sure I recognise you from the newspapers and have read of your many exploits, but your name is not familiar.'

Charlie was quick to explain. 'Earl Montgomery is His Royal Highness Sultan Kadir Al Sulaimar of Zenhab.'

Lexi ignored her future brother-in-law as her eyes locked with the Sultan's. 'Should I address you as Your Royal Highness or My Lord?' she asked, mockingly deferential. She saw amusement and something darker and more dangerous in his intent gaze. The air between them was charged with an electrical current that made every nerve ending on Lexi's body tingle.

'I insist that you call me Kadir, Lexi.' His sexy accent lingered on each syllable of her name. He smiled, showing his white teeth, and a quiver shot through Lexi as she imagined him nipping her throat and the soft flesh of her earlobe. 'I find it is unwise to believe everything printed in the newspapers,' he murmured. 'So often, stories are reported incorrectly or are blatantly untrue.'

'That's a little unfair to journalists. I'm sure most press reports are properly researched and presented.' She thought of all those women who had revealed intimate details of their affairs with His Royal Hotness. Some of the stories must be true.

The sound of a gong rang through the ballroom, shattering the tense atmosphere.

'Charlie and I are supposed to lead everyone into the dining room for the buffet,' Athena explained. She slipped her arm through her fiancé's and promptly tripped on the hem of her long skirt, earning an impatient tut from Charles Fairfax.

Kadir offered his arm to Lexi. 'May I escort you to dinner?'

It was impossible to refuse without causing a scene, but she glared at him as she placed her hand stiffly on his arm and he drew her closer so that her thigh brushed against his as they walked into the dining room.

'How dare you...*infiltrate* my sister's engagement party,' she hissed.

His wide shoulders shook with laughter. 'It would have been bad manners to refuse an invitation from an old school friend.'

'You didn't worry about manners when you came on to me while your girlfriend—with emphasis on the word *girl*—was in the next room.' That wiped the smug smile from his face, she noted with satisfaction.

He dipped his head close to hers. 'Let's get something straight.' His voice was suddenly harsh. The charismatic playboy prince had disappeared and Lexi had a sense that Sultan Kadir Al Sulaimar was a powerful man and a dangerous threat to her peace of mind. 'I did not invite Tania Stewart to my suite and definitely not into my bed. I was as surprised as you were when she walked out of the bedroom.'

Lexi wondered why she believed him. 'Not that I care how you conduct your private life, or with whom, but, out of curiosity, how was Tania in your room if you didn't invite her in?'

'She admitted she'd taken the pass key from the cleaner's office. Her father owns the hotel and she knows where things are kept. When you saw her you immediately leapt to the conclusion that she and I were lovers.'

'She *was* naked under that sheet,' Lexi defended herself. She found she was unable to tear her eyes from Kadir's smouldering gaze.

'Forget Tania. This is about you and me.'

'There is no *you and me*!' She wished she could control her racing pulse. 'I'm not the slightest bit interested in you, Earl Montgomery, or Sultan of Zenhab, or whatever other fancy title I'm supposed to call you.'

'Kadir,' he said softly. 'Why are you uptight about saying my name?'

'I'm *not* uptight.' Glancing around her, Lexi flushed when she realised that her raised voice had attracted curious glances from the other guests.

The amused gleam in his eyes told her he was aware that she felt churned up inside and quite unlike her usual self. 'Perhaps later tonight we will have a chance to discuss my proposition.'

'I've told you I'm not interested in your proposition.'

'How do you know, when you don't know what it is?'

'Knowing of your reputation as a playboy, I have no qualms about turning down your proposition without hearing any of the sordid details,' Lexi said tartly.

Satisfied that she'd had the last word, she turned her back on him and began to select food from the buffet even though her appetite had disappeared. To her relief, Charlie returned to monopolise Kadir's attention and she was able to slip away to a quiet corner and forced down a couple of vol-au-vents filled with a cream cheese mixture that tasted overpoweringly of chopped herbs.

She brooded on her conversation with her sister. Athena—like the coastguard commander, Roger Norris—had accused her of putting up barriers to prevent people getting too close to her. It wasn't deliberate, but subconsciously, perhaps, her wariness of being rejected *did* make her appear remote and self-contained, Lexi acknowledged. She had learned from a young age that the only person she could rely on, the only person she could trust, was herself. When she had served with the RAF she'd learned to trust the professionalism of the people she worked with. But when she *had* lowered her guard with Steven Cromer and followed her heart instead of her head, his rejection had been hurtful and humiliating; she was in no hurry to experience either of those emotions again.

Waiters were circling the room offering glasses of champagne to toast the newly engaged couple. Lexi opted for iced water, hoping she would soon be able to slip away from the party and drive to West London, where she had arranged to stay at a friend's flat while she looked for another job. She sipped the water, but her throat still felt dry and scratchy and the headache that had started five minutes ago was rapidly becoming worse.

Lord Fairfax called for silence and proceeded to give a lengthy speech about how delighted he and his wife were to announce their son's engagement. Lady Fairfax's delight was not apparent on her haughty features, Lexi noted. Charlie looked bored and Athena was tense and had spilled something down the front of her dress.

'What does your sister see in an oaf like Charles Fairfax, apart from his money and title?' The husky drawl close to her ear brought a flush of heat to Lexi's face. She shot Kadir a glowering look and winced as the sudden movement sent a shooting pain through her skull.

'Athena isn't like that,' she said curtly, not about to admit to a stranger her own doubts about her sister's choice of husband. 'She loves Charlie.' She frowned. 'I thought he was your friend. Why else would you accept an invitation to his engagement party?'

'I knew you would be here.'

He was serious, Lexi realised. The smouldering sensuality in Kadir's eyes made her catch her breath. She looked away from him and tried to control her frantic heartbeat. But her chest felt constricted and her shortness of breath was not entirely down to her acute awareness of him. In the last few minutes she had begun to feel nauseous and strangely lightheaded, as if she was drunk, except that she hadn't had a drop of alcohol all evening. She swayed on legs that suddenly seemed unable to support her.

'Are you all right? You've gone a strange colour.' Kadir's voice sounded from a long way off. Lexi closed her eyes to stop the room from spinning. She could feel beads of sweat on her brow, and she suddenly knew what was wrong with her. To her horror, she realised that she was going to be sick in front of a room full of onlookers.

She blinked and Kadir's handsome face swam before her eyes. He was the last person she would turn to for help, but she was feeling worse by the second and she had no choice but to abandon her pride. 'Please,' she muttered. 'Please…get me out of here.'

He gave her a sharp look and growled something beneath his breath, then the room spun, Lexi's head spun, as he scooped her up into his arms. She sensed everyone was watching them as Kadir strode past the curious guests and she heard Charlie Fairfax say loudly, 'She's obviously had too much to drink.' Kadir tightened his arms around her and Lexi, who had never been carried by a man in her entire adult life, rested her head on his chest and listened to the steady thud of his heart.

Athena dashed into the hall after them, looking anxious. 'Lexi… Lady Fairfax has just told me that the vol-au-vent filling contained prawns. You didn't eat any, did you?'

'Unfortunately, your warning is too late,' Lexi muttered drily. Noticing Kadir's puzzled expression, she explained, 'I have a shellfish allergy.' Her voice became urgent. 'I need to get to a bathroom—*quickly*.'

At first, when Lexi opened her eyes and did not recognise her surroundings, she wondered if she was in a bedroom at the Fairfax home, Woodley Lodge. Vague snatches of memory floated into her mind of sitting in a car and travelling very fast. She remembered that the car had stopped at least once and she had been ill by the side of the road.

There were other memories of strong arms around her, supporting her while she had been sick, a cool hand stroking her hair back from her hot brow.

Where the hell was she? Ignoring the fact that she felt like a limp rag, Lexi sat up and froze as she pushed back the sheets and discovered that someone had removed her dress, leaving her in her sheer lace black bra and matching thong.

Kadir had rescued her from the ignominy of being ill in front of the guests at her sister's engagement party. Had he driven her to wherever this place was—a hotel, perhaps— and undressed her? She glanced around the bedroom, noting the floral wallpaper and an oil painting of a horse hanging above the antique dressing table. The décor of slightly old-fashioned elegance did not feel like she was in a hotel.

Her legs felt weak when she made the short journey into the en suite bathroom and a glance in the mirror revealed that she looked as washed out as she felt. There was a toothbrush among the toiletries on the vanity unit and she felt marginally better once she'd brushed her teeth and pulled a comb through her hair. Walking back into the bedroom, she stopped dead and stared wordlessly at Kadir.

'I knocked but you didn't answer, so I thought I'd better check on you.' His dark eyes drifted over her, bringing a tinge of colour to Lexi's wan face. 'How are you feeling?'

Vulnerable, but no way would she admit it to him. 'Better.' She instinctively crossed her arms over her breasts, wishing she had pulled on the towelling robe that she'd noticed hanging on the bathroom door. 'At the risk of sounding like a corny line from a film, where am I?'

'My English home, Montgomery Manor. Windsor is less than half an hour's drive from Henley-on-Thames, although it took longer to get here last night because you needed me to pull over a couple of times.'

Lexi felt mortified that he had seen her at her most undignified, throwing up in a gutter.

'Did you undress me?' she asked curtly. She had a hazy recollection of being carried up a flight of stairs and placed on a bed, and she remembered feeling her zip being drawn down her spine and the sensation of cool air on her body as her dress was removed.

'There you go, jumping to conclusions again, like you did about Tania,' Kadir said mockingly, but Lexi heard anger in his tone. 'You were so ill you couldn't even walk. Do you think I took advantage of your defenceless state to strip you…and do what—look at you, touch you?'

She bit her lip. 'I had a particularly bad reaction to shellfish last night. I don't remember much after you carried me out of the Fairfaxes' house. All I know is that someone took my dress off. I recall that someone stayed with me and gave me some water.' Someone had slipped an arm around her and held a glass of water to her lips. She remembered gentle hands wiping a cool flannel over her feverish brow.

'My housekeeper put you into bed and took your dress away to be cleaned.' He shrugged. 'I called my doctor and explained your symptoms, and he advised me to stay with you until you'd stopped being sick.' His jaw hardened. 'Believe me, helping you to the bathroom a dozen times did not send me into a frenzy of sexual excitement.'

Kadir watched a stain of colour run along her high cheekbones and some of his anger abated. There were dark circles beneath her eyes and she looked fragile, but he sensed she would hate showing any sign of weakness. He had never met a woman who infuriated and intrigued him as much as Lexi Howard did.

It was a long time since he had been so turned on by a woman, he acknowledged. He was even beginning to question his plans to employ the Flight Captain as his private pilot. But the truth was that she was exactly what he needed and he would have to ignore his inconvenient throb of desire and try to forget that the uptight Ms Howard had a penchant for skimpy, sexy underwear.

Last night, when she had been sick for hour after hour, he had been more concerned about persuading her to take sips of water to prevent her from becoming dehydrated, as the doctor had instructed, and he'd barely noticed that she was almost naked.

But he noticed now.

When she had emerged from the bathroom, his eyes had been drawn to her nipples, clearly visible through her bra, and the shadow of blonde hair beneath the tiny triangle of semi-transparent material between her legs. He had been right about her wearing stockings. They were held up by wide bands of black lace around the tops of her thighs. Kadir's pulse quickened and he dragged his eyes from her, feeling like a voyeur, or an excited teenage boy seeing a naked woman for the first time.

In a bid to ease the throb of his arousal he walked over to the window and pretended to be fascinated by the view of Windsor Great Park.

'Your dress isn't ready yet,' he said abruptly, 'so I brought one of my shirts for you to wear. It's on the bed.'

'Thank you.' Lexi hurried across the room and snatched up the shirt. It was much too big, and as she did up the buttons she felt marginally less exposed now that her underwear was hidden. She had only worn a seamless bra and thong so that they wouldn't show under her clingy dress. Kadir would have completely the wrong idea about her. She wasn't a flighty, flirty type of woman who dressed to impress men. She was sensible, serious—*boring*, taunted a little voice inside her head.

'As a matter of fact, all my clothes are in the boot of my car. After the party, I'd planned to drive to London to stay at a friend's flat.'

'I sent a couple of my staff over to Woodley Lodge to pick up your car.'

'Thank you,' Lexi repeated stiffly. 'I'm sorry to be such a nuisance.'

She looked across the room to where he was standing, half turned away from her so that she could see his proud profile. A weakness invaded her limbs that had nothing to do with her being ill the previous night. Dressed in faded jeans that moulded his firm thighs and buttocks and a cream cashmere sweater that accentuated his exotic olive-gold skin, he was the epitome of masculine perfection. Any woman would find him attractive, she consoled herself. Nevertheless, it was irritating to realise that she was no different to those women in the tabloids who had proudly described every intimate detail of their affairs with the playboy prince of the desert.

She thought about how he had stayed with her during the previous night and taken care of her when she had been ill. Perhaps there was more to him than his reputation as a jet-setting philanderer gave him credit for.

'Thanks for rescuing me from the party last night,' she said awkwardly. 'I guess that makes us even.'

'It's hardly the same thing. You saved my life.' Kadir swung round and gave her a brooding look. 'In fact, events have worked in my favour because now you are trapped here in my home, which gives us an opportunity to discuss my proposition.'

Needing a distraction from the realisation that without her car or clothes she could not leave Montgomery Manor, Lexi asked curiously, 'How are you an English Earl *and* the Sultan of Zenhab?'

'My mother is English. She met my father when he came to England to buy a racehorse from the Montgomery stud farm, and after a whirlwind courtship she married him and went to Zenhab as his Sultana. Unfortunately, my mother wasn't cut out for life in a remote desert kingdom far away from Bond Street,' Kadir said drily. 'My parents split up when I was seven and I continued to live with my father, but I visited my mother and grandparents regularly and went to school in England. When my grandfather, the tenth Earl, died, the title and estate passed to me. However, I do not spend as much time here as perhaps I should. It was my destiny to rule Zenhab.'

But there was a price to his destiny, Kadir thought heavily. To claim the Crown from his uncle, he had been forced to agree to an arranged marriage. His jaw clenched. It was time for him to honour his promise. This trip to Europe would be his last as a single man, and on his return to Zenhab he would set a date for his wedding.

The prospect felt like a lead weight inside him. He tried telling himself that most men faced with imminent marriage, even to a woman they loved, would feel a sense of panic. He did not love his future bride; he had never met her. But until three days ago he had been resigned to fulfilling his duty.

Why was it that since he had met Lexi Howard he had felt a sense that prison bars were closing around him, sealing his fate? Perhaps it was because she was off-limits. He had never denied himself a woman before, he thought derisively. Maybe the knowledge that he could not allow the simmering sexual chemistry that existed between them to ignite was the reason for the raw feeling inside him, the curious longing for something he could not define or explain.

He stared unseeingly out of the window while he struggled to bring his emotions under control. His desire for Lexi was irrelevant. It had occurred to him that it would be a good idea to employ a female helicopter pilot to fly his future bride around Zenhab. He knew that Haleema would only be permitted to travel to the palace accompanied by a chaperone, meaning that he would have no chance to meet privately the woman with whom he must spend the rest of his life.

Employing a female helicopter pilot would negate the necessity for Haleema to have a chaperone, and perhaps there might be an opportunity for him to establish a rapport with the princess of the mountain tribes who would rule Zenhab with him and bear his children.

He swung round, and his eyes were as hard as his heart as he stared at Lexi. 'The proposition that I want to discuss with you is this. I want you to come to Zenhab and work for me as my private helicopter pilot.'

CHAPTER FIVE

HE WANTED HER to be his pilot! Lexi's face grew
warm as she recalled how she had put a very
different interpretation on Kadir's proposition.
In her wild imagination she had even thought
that he might suggest that they become lovers. Desperate to hide her embarrassment, she
said crisply, 'Why me? You must have pilots
in Zenhab.'

'Of course, but none of the military pilots
who belong to the royal household are trained
to fly the model of helicopter that I have
bought. What I'm proposing is a six-month
contract, during which time you will be my
personal pilot and driver, and you will also in-
struct pilots from the Zenhabian air force on
how to fly the AgustaWestland.

'You are ideal for the job,' Kadir insisted.
'Initially, when you joined the RAF, you were
a chauffeur for the Commanding Officer of
an air force base before you went on to train

as a pilot. You flew an AW169 for the coast-guard agency and know the helicopter inside out. In Afghanistan you were awarded a Distinguished Flying Cross for rescuing injured soldiers under fire.'

'You've certainly done your homework,' she said drily.

More than she knew, Kadir mused. Apart from her impressive military record, his security team had dug up a few other interesting facts about her, including the fact that she owed a significant amount of money to various credit card companies. The first time he had met her, he had formed the opinion that Lexi Howard liked to be in control. The news that she had money problems had surprised him, but it worked in his favour.

'Naturally, the salary I am prepared to pay will reflect your flying experience and expertise.'

The figure Kadir named made Lexi blink. Her job with the coastguard agency had been well paid, but she hadn't earned in a year what Kadir was offering for six months' work. The money was tempting, she acknowledged, because it would allow her to pay off the debts that her birth mother had accrued.

Lexi thought of the woman who had given her away when she had been a few days old.

Ten years ago, with the help of the adoption agency, she had found her birth mother. But her dream of an emotional reunion had been disappointing. Cathy Barnes had bluntly admitted that she had been a teenager when she had given birth to Lexi, but she hadn't wanted a baby. *'I don't know your father's name. I didn't ask names. I just met clients in hotel rooms and they paid me for what they wanted. They were mostly businessmen with fat expense accounts to blow.'*

Lexi still remembered how shocked she had felt when Cathy had revealed that she had been working as a prostitute when she had fallen pregnant.

A few years after she had given Lexi up for adoption Cathy had married, but to this day she had never told her husband that she had a daughter.

It was painful for Lexi to know that she was her birth mother's shameful secret. She met Cathy sporadically and their relationship was friendly rather than close. But six months ago Cathy had revealed that she had terminal cancer and had broken down as she'd explained that her husband was unaware that she owed a fortune on credit cards. Seeing her mother's distress had tugged on Lexi's heart, especially as Cathy did not have long to live. To spare her mother further worry, she had arranged for the debts to be transferred onto her own credit card.

'What is your answer? I don't believe you will find a better job offer than mine.' Kadir's voice tugged Lexi's mind back to the present.

She couldn't disagree with him—it was a darned good job offer, and she needed a job. So why was she hesitating?

She had a sudden flashback to those moments in his hotel suite when he had almost kissed her. The spicy scent of his aftershave had intoxicated her senses, just as it was doing now, she thought. Her nerves jangled as she watched him walk towards her, and her heart thudded erratically as her eyes were drawn to his mouth and she remembered the taste of his warm breath on her lips.

A quiver of sexual desire shot through her body, so intense that it took her breath away. She did not want to want him, and she certainly did not want him to finish what he had started at his hotel, she assured herself.

'My new helicopter was manufactured here in England and is ready for collection,' Kadir explained. 'I plan to be in Europe for another week to attend a number of business meetings before I return to Zenhab.'

'The AW doesn't have the range to fly long-haul.'

'A plane from my Royal Fleet will transport the chopper to Zenhab. I assume you are able to start work immediately?'

'I haven't actually agreed to take the job,' Lexi reminded him.

He assumed way too much, she thought as she watched his heavy brows snap together in a frown. It seemed safe to assume that the Sultan was used to having his own way. 'What about accommodation in Zenhab?' she asked abruptly. 'Where would I live?'

'At the royal palace. I will need you to be available at all times.'

Lexi was annoyed when she felt herself blush, and she wondered if Kadir was deliberately playing with words to make her feel flustered.

'You will be allocated a suite of rooms at the palace with access to a private garden and pool, and my staff will do their utmost to fulfil all your needs. All you will have to do is fly my helicopter, and spend a lot of time relaxing in the Zenhabian sunshine. You know, I can't help thinking that maybe we got off to a bad start,' Kadir murmured.

Lexi's brows lifted. 'Whatever gave you that idea?' she said drily.

His mouth crooked into a sensual smile that caused the heat inside Lexi to burn hotter.

'Can we start again—as friends? I've seen that you are an excellent pilot, and I would very much like you to work for me, Lexi.'

She would be a fool to turn this job and high salary down. All she had to do was spend six months in his desert kingdom—at a royal palace. How hard could it be compared to a dusty military camp in Afghanistan? Lexi asked herself. A traitorous thought slid into her head that the palace staff could not fulfil *all* her needs—followed by the even more treacherous thought that undoubtedly the playboy Sultan *could*!

But she would never be any man's plaything. She would never be a rich man's whore like her birth mother had been.

Whatever had happened in the past, Cathy needed her now, Lexi reminded herself. Had she offered to help her birth mother because she subconsciously hoped that Cathy would love her enough so that she would publicly recognise the daughter she had kept secret for nearly thirty years? Deep inside Lexi there was still the little girl who had studied a family photograph and wondered why she looked so different to her parents and baby sister. That had been the day she had learned she was adopted, and even at the age of five she had understood that she was on her own.

She lifted her head and met Kadir's deep brown gaze, determined not to melt beneath his charismatic smile.

'I'm confident that we can have a mutually respectful relationship, Your Highness,' she said coolly. 'I accept your offer.'

A week later, as Lexi lowered herself into the turquoise pool on the rooftop of Kadir's luxury penthouse apartment in Monaco, she reflected that there were certainly benefits to working for a billionaire. The view of the Mediterranean sparkling in the early morning sunshine was breathtaking, and at this time of the day she had the pool to herself. Not that any of the other members of Kadir's entourage were likely to use the pool, she mused. His two bodyguards kept themselves to themselves, and the elderly manservant Walif, when he was not attending to his master's needs, or viewing Lexi with deep suspicion, was often to be found dozing in an armchair.

She wondered what time Kadir had returned to the penthouse, or whether the party he had attended aboard a Russian oligarch's yacht had gone on all night. Lexi frowned, remembering the gorgeous bikini-clad women who had been gathered on Boris Denisov's super-yacht moored in Monaco's harbour. Like the other 'business meetings' Kadir had attended at the Folies Bergère in Paris and the prestigious Caves du Roy nightclub in St Tropez earlier in the week, she doubted he had spent much time discussing commercial deals when he'd been surrounded by all that naked, nubile flesh.

'There's no need for you to wait for me,' he had told her last night as he'd stepped out of the car onto the jetty and waved to the eager reception committee on the Russian's yacht. 'I'll make my own way back to the penthouse.'

'Are you sure you'll have the energy?' Lexi had murmured drily, earning her one of Kadir's outrageously sexy smiles that had a predictable effect on her heart-rate. Her gaze had been drawn to the girls on the yacht, with their golden tans and itsy-bitsy bikinis, and she had felt staid and inexplicably angry with herself, life and, top of the list, His Royal Rake—prince of the one-night stand!

It was partly her own fault she felt a frump, Lexi acknowledged. Before they had left England Kadir had chosen a pilot's uniform out of a catalogue for her to wear, which had consisted of an eye-wateringly short skirt and a tight-fitting jacket.

'I presume you're joking,' she'd said disgustedly. 'I'm a pilot, not a *Playboy* centrefold.' She had ordered a smart grey suit with a sensible mid-calf-length skirt, much to Kadir's amusement. He seemed to find her a joke and the more she treated him with icy politeness, the more he teased her and tried to draw a reaction from her. Over the past week a battle of wills had developed between them, and Kadir's weapons of choice were his laid-back charm and his sexy smile that Lexi suspected he was fully aware turned her insides to marshmallow.

She did not understand why she was letting him get to her, or why the wicked gleam in his eyes and his husky laughter when she gave him a withering look bothered her so much. She realised he was playing a game and she had no intention of taking his flirtatious behaviour seriously. But that did not stop her heart from thudding whenever he was near—and as he insisted on sitting next to her when she flew the helicopter, and he occupied the front passenger seat when she chauffeured him in the limousine, her nerves seemed to be permanently on edge.

Forcing her mind away from the man who disturbed her equilibrium, Lexi checked the strings of her halter-neck bikini were securely tied. The silver bikini had been a crazy impulse buy after she had dropped Kadir at the marina. The three tiny triangles of material revealed more of her body than she was comfortable with, and the bikini was not as practical to swim in as the navy one-piece she usually wore. Cursing her stupidity, she struck out through the cool water and swam twenty lengths of the pool, hoping that strenuous exercise would ease the restless ache in her limbs.

She surfaced after completing the final length and shook her wet hair back from her face.

'You look like a water nymph.'

The husky drawl caused her heart to collide with her ribcage and she sucked in a swift breath as she looked up and saw Kadir sprawled on a sun lounger. His bow tie was undone, and so were several of his shirt buttons, affording Lexi a glimpse of his naked chest covered in whorls of black hairs. The night's growth of dark stubble shading his jaw accentuated his lethal sensuality. She had no idea how long he had been watching her. He moved with the silent stealth of a jungle cat, she thought irritably.

She arched her brows. 'Have you met many nymphs? I would have thought that you'd have your hands full with real women, without concerning yourself with mythological ones.'

He laughed softly and the sound sent a curl of heat through Lexi. 'What a delightful picture you paint. I can visualise myself with my hands full of women.'

One woman, if he was truthful, Kadir mused. He had been on his way to bed, and had stepped onto the rooftop patio for some much needed fresh air after the fug of cloying perfume and cigar smoke that had filled Boris Denisov's yacht. But the sight of Lexi wearing a sexy bikini, with her long blonde hair streaming down her back, had made him forget that he was tired after many hours of negotiations, during which he had persuaded the Russian oligarch to invest in a business venture worth billions of pounds to Zenhab's economy.

Kadir let his gaze drift over Lexi's slender body and her high, firm breasts, and the slow burn of desire that had simmered in his gut since he had first set eyes on her grew hotter and more intense. For the past week, she had driven him mad with her frosty attitude and sharp, often sarcastic, wit, her lack of deference for his royal status. Oh, she was polite, but he had a sense that she had judged him and found him wanting, and Kadir was finding it increasingly hard to resist the challenge in her cool blue gaze.

'I trust your business meeting was successful?' she murmured. 'By the way, you have lipstick on your collar.'

'The night was very satisfactory.' Kadir tucked his hands behind his head, thinking of the agreement he'd got from Boris to build a luxury hotel complex which would attract tourists to Zenhab.

Lexi pursed her lips. Had he had sex with the strumpet who had left a scarlet imprint of her lips on his white shirt? Maybe he'd had more than one woman last night. Probably— knowing his reputation. Acid burned in her stomach and she told herself she must have swallowed some of the chlorine in the pool. Kadir was lying back on the lounger, watching her through half-closed eyes. He looked indolent and beautiful and Lexi had never been more aware of a man in her life. *Why him—a man she did not even like, let alone respect?*

'I wonder what the Zenhabian people think of their Sultan who, as far as I can tell, spends more time partying and living up to his playboy reputation than trying to improve the lives of many of the population who live in poverty?' she said tartly. 'I've heard that your father devoted his life to establishing peace and security in the kingdom, but clearly you don't share his sense of duty.'

'What do you know about my country, and

why do you care about my people?' Kadir demanded, stung by her comments. Duty and the desire to ensure long-term stability in Zenhab had made him agree to an arranged marriage with a girl who his weasel of an uncle had chosen for him, he thought bitterly. Lexi had overstepped the mark this time.

He was tempted to point out that many of the best business deals were made through networking and at social events. More deals were arranged over drinks at a bar than around a boardroom table. But he could imagine the response he would get if he told Miss Prim and Proper that he had been hard at work at last night's party.

'I've been reading about the history of Zenhab,' Lexi told him. 'After all, I am going to be living and working in the kingdom for a few months.'

'You would do well to remember that I am your employer,' Kadir said curtly, 'and I suggest you keep your opinions to yourself.'

'I'll try to remember that, Your Highness.' Lexi did not recognise the devil inside who seemed hell-bent on antagonising Kadir. She could tell she had angered him. His lazy smile had disappeared and the sensual gleam in his chocolate-brown eyes had been replaced with a hard stare that riled her, even though she acknowledged that she'd had no right to criticise him.

'While we are on the subject of your employment, I have a special assignment for you.' Kadir got to his feet and walked to the edge of the pool, meaning that Lexi had to tilt her head to look at his face. 'Later today you will fly us to Lake Como in Italy, to the home of a good friend of mine, Conte Luca De Rossi. Luca is hosting a business dinner and an American entrepreneur who I am hoping to do business with will be there.' Kadir hesitated for a nanosecond. 'I want you to be my companion for the evening.'

Lexi stared at him. 'I know nothing about business.'

'You don't have to know anything.' Again he paused and, to Lexi's surprise, he appeared almost awkward. 'I need you to be my date.'

'Your *date*?' Her eyebrows almost disappeared beneath her hairline.

'It's not difficult to understand,' Kadir said impatiently.

'Excuse me, but it is when I bet that any of the women you met last night would be gagging to be your date. Why is it important for you to take a partner to the dinner, anyway?'

He exhaled heavily. 'The American businessman, Chuck Weinberg, is bringing his nineteen-year-old daughter. I met Danielle a few months ago when I visited Chuck's home in Texas.' Kadir grimaced. 'Danielle is a very determined young woman who is used to getting what she wants…and she made it clear that she wants me. To be frank, I want to concentrate on discussing my business proposition with Chuck without having to fend off his daughter.'

'Yes, I can see how annoying that would be,' Lexi said in a cool tone that failed to disguise her boiling anger. She gave in to the childish impulse and splashed water over Kadir's designer suit, before she dived beneath the water and swam to the far end of the pool.

He had a nerve! She was so furious that she could feel her heart jumping up and down in her chest. *Why was she so stupid?* Lexi's anger was partly directed at herself. For a moment, when Kadir had asked her to be his date, she'd thought it was a serious invitation and he genuinely wanted her to accompany him to the dinner party.

Glancing over her shoulder, she saw him stride into the penthouse. She had conveniently forgotten that he'd said he wanted her to carry out an assignment. Now she knew that he wanted her to be his paid escort. She rested her arms on the side of the pool and stared over the rooftops at the sea in the distance. The bright sparkle of the sun on the waves made her eyes water—at least that was what she told herself. With an impatient gesture she dashed her hand over her damp eyelashes.

Her birth mother had been an escort. *It sounds classier than call girl*, Cathy had told Lexi when she had spoken about how she had been drawn into prostitution to fund her drug habit.

Lost in her thoughts, Lexi gave a startled cry when a muscular arm curled around her waist and she was half lifted out of the water as Kadir turned her round to face him.

'What's the matter with you?' he growled. 'I made a simple request...'

'You asked me to pretend to be your mistress. I don't call that a simple request; I call that a darned cheek!' With her face mere inches from his naked bronzed chest, Lexi numbly realised that while he had been inside the apartment he had changed into his swimming shorts.

Her heart kicked into life as she jerked her eyes back to his face to find him watching her intently. She licked her dry lips and his dark gaze focused on the tip of her tongue. The cool water lapped her hot breasts and she felt her nipples harden to taut peaks that chafed against her clingy bikini bra. She was standing with her back against the wall of the pool and Kadir placed his arms on either side of her body, caging her in.

'Nowhere in my contract does it state that one of my duties is to masquerade as your mistress to protect you from the clutches of women who want to climb into your bed,' she said fiercely. 'I don't want to pretend to be your dinner date and I doubt I could convince anyone that we have an intimate relationship.'

'Intimate,' Kadir murmured, his voice suddenly as sensual as molten syrup. 'I like the way that sounds. Don't underestimate yourself, Lexi. I'm sure you could be a very convincing mistress.'

Too late, Lexi recognised the danger she was in. 'Take your hands off me.' In a distant corner of her mind she knew she sounded like a Victorian maiden. What had happened to her military training? she asked herself impatiently. She brought her knee up swiftly between Kadir's legs, but he was quicker and trapped her leg between his thighs. Tension thrummed between them and the only sound was her own quickened breathing.

Deep down, Lexi acknowledged that she had been goading him since he'd arrived at the pool; since the moment she'd first met him, if she was honest. Now, as he lowered his head his eyes reflected the challenge in hers.

'It's not my hands you need to worry about,' he drawled. And then he brought his mouth down on hers and the world exploded.

He was merciless, taking advantage of her cry of protest to thrust his tongue between her lips and explore her with mind-blowing eroticism. Lexi had never been kissed like that in her life, hadn't known that a kiss could be so hot and dark and shockingly wicked. Any idea she'd had of trying to resist him was swept away by his shimmering sexual hunger. He crushed her mouth beneath his and demanded everything: her soul, her secret fantasies, her total capitulation to his mastery. She had dared to challenge him with her cool blue eyes and Kadir would show her that the desert king *never* refused a challenge.

Lexi's body burned with an intensity of need that made a mockery of her belief that she did not have a high sex drive. She had assumed that she was not a particularly sensual person and, although she was not a virgin, her previous sexual experiences had left her with a vague sense of disappointment and bemusement that sonnets had been written about something frankly so mundane.

Everything she thought she knew about herself was shattered by the white-hot desire that ripped through her. Kadir was not touching her body, only her mouth, as he crushed her lips beneath his and deepened the kiss, and Lexi sank into darkness and heat and danger. Compelled by an instinct as old as womankind, she pushed her hips forward, urgently seeking contact with his pelvis.

He should not have started this. The realisation drummed a warning in Kadir's brain. What had begun as a lesson designed to show Lexi that *he* was in command was rapidly becoming a test of his will power. She was so responsive, so hungry, meeting his demands with demands of her own and with a boldness that he should have expected from the strong woman he knew her to be. But he could not take what he so desperately wanted. He should not have made the ice maiden melt and he could not allow himself to burn in her fire. The temptation to sink into her yielding softness and rest his thighs on hers nearly broke his resolve.

Who would know if he enjoyed one last fling before he returned to Zenhab and the life of duty that awaited him?

He would know, Kadir thought grimly. He heard his father's voice inside his head. *To cheat others requires you to cheat yourself first, and who can respect a cheat?*

He wrenched his mouth from Lexi's, feeling ashamed of his weakness and his inability to resist her. She had responded to him, he reminded himself. He was not solely to blame. But the best way he could ensure that the situation never happened again was to fire up her hot temper.

'Remember, when we are sitting at the dinner table tonight with Luca and his guests, I'll be remembering how your tongue felt inside my mouth. Remember that I know your secret, Lexi.'

'What secret?' Lexi dragged oxygen into her lungs and forced her lips, stinging from Kadir's kiss, to form the question.

Kadir deliberately dropped his gaze to her pebble-hard nipples jutting provocatively through her bikini top and his satisfied smile made Lexi's skin prickle with shame. 'We both know I could have you. Did you buy your tiny bikini and imagine me untying the straps that hold it together? Perhaps I should take you here and now, and at the dinner party there will be no need for you to pretend that you are my mistress?'

Heat blazed on her cheeks. 'I don't have to listen to this. I certainly don't have to put up with being mauled by my employer. I resign,' Lexi told him furiously.

'You would walk away from the best-paid job you are likely to find because your pride has taken a knock? I didn't have you down as a coward, Lexi. I thought you had more guts.'

'I am *not* a coward.'

He shrugged. 'There is also the matter of a financial penalty if you break your contract.'

She had signed a contract which had made her a member of the royal staff, and she would owe him three months' salary if she left before completing six months' service. Lexi knew she could not afford to take on any more debt. 'A few thousand pounds is nothing to you,' she said bitterly.

She dragged her eyes from his exquisitely chiselled features and stared at his hands gripping the edge of the pool on either side of her. She had accused him of mauling her, but he had not actually touched her body. The knowledge that he had set her on fire simply with a kiss compounded her humiliation.

Kadir's knuckles were white, and Lexi had the strange sense that he was holding on to the edge of the pool as if his life depended on it. The muscles of his forearms and shoulders were bunched as if he was under intolerable tension and he was breathing hard, his big chest rising and falling jerkily, matching the frantic rhythm of her own heartbeat. She looked into his eyes, expecting to see mockery, but the hard brilliance in his gaze revealed a hunger that shocked her. The realisation that this was not a game to him scared her as much as it excited her.

'Release me from my contract. Let me go before this gets out of hand,' she pleaded in a low, shaken voice.

Logic told Kadir she was right. Taking Lexi to Zenhab would be madness now that he had tasted her. What had started out as a challenge—to melt her ice—had changed irrevocably now that he had discovered her heat and softness and incandescent sensuality.

But the fact remained that he wanted to employ a female helicopter pilot to fly his intended bride around Zenhab. His desire for Lexi was an inconvenience that he would have to deal with, Kadir told himself firmly. His life was mapped out and the path he must take had been plotted by his uncle Jamal. For stability in Zenhab, and for the promise he'd made to his father, he would marry the bride who had been chosen for him.

'We will leave for Italy at two o'clock,' he said abruptly, dropping his arms to his sides, his fists clenched as if he couldn't trust himself not to reach for Lexi's slender body and pull her into the heat of him, the need that burned bright and fierce in his gut.

In a dignified silence that somehow simmered with fury, she climbed the steps leading out of the pool, water streaming from her limbs and her long white-gold hair. Kadir watched her walk into the penthouse and cursed savagely before he ducked beneath the surface of the pool and powered through the water.

Lexi did not look round, did not even stop to snatch up her towel as she ran inside and almost collided with Kadir's manservant. Walif—as she had come to expect—did not speak to her, but she sensed his disapproval and, when she hurried into her bedroom and glanced in the mirror, the sight of her swollen lips, reddened from Kadir's kiss, brought a flush to her face and strengthened her resolve to keep her relationship with the Sultan of Zenhab on strictly professional lines from now on.

CHAPTER SIX

HIS LAST NIGHT of freedom!

It was not quite as dramatic as that, Kadir acknowledged, the corners of his mouth lifting in a wry smile of self-derision. A royal wedding would take months to arrange, and technically he was free until he led his new bride into his private bedchamber and they were alone for the first time.

But this evening would be his last in Europe for many months, until after his wedding to Haleema had taken place. What better place to be than at Conte Luca De Rossi's breathtaking villa on the shores of Lake Como?

Kadir was grateful to his old school friend for arranging the dinner party and inviting Chuck Weinberg. The American businessman had seemed enthusiastic about investing in the developing telecommunications industry in Zenhab during initial discussions that had taken place in Texas. Tonight, Kadir planned to utilise all his persuasive skills to hopefully secure a deal that would bring his desert kingdom fully into the twenty-first century.

There was only one problem—and she was making a beeline for him across the magnificent entrance hall of the Villa De Rossi. Danielle Weinberg had big hair, a big smile and big breasts that Kadir, who had a certain amount of hands-on experience of the female anatomy, was certain owed more to a cosmetic surgeon's skill than to genetics.

'Kad*eer*, I've been looking all over for you.'

She reminded Kadir of an over-enthusiastic puppy. As he gently but firmly unlocked Danielle's hands from around his neck, he was struck by the thought that his future bride was a similar age to the young American. His jaw clenched. In Zenhab a life of duty awaited him, but tonight he was determined to enjoy his last few hours of freedom.

Despite what he had told Lexi, he knew he could handle Danielle with the same diplomacy that he dealt with her father. But when he had asked Lexi to partner him at the dinner party he had lost his nerve—something that had *never* happened to Kadir before. Citing Danielle as an excuse had seemed like a good idea, but it had backfired spectacularly, and had led to him kissing Lexi in what had started out as a punishment and ended in searing passion that he knew he should not have allowed to happen. His behaviour had been inappropriate, and Lexi had made him aware of that fact on the helicopter flight from Monaco to the Villa De Rossi, when she had been as cold as a Siberian winter.

Kadir glanced at his watch. She was late coming down for dinner. His mouth tightened with annoyance as he remembered her excuse that she had nothing suitable to wear to a grand dinner party. Would she wear the evening gown he had arranged to be delivered to her room? He would give her five more minutes before he went to find her, and if necessary he would put the damned dress on her!

His attention was drawn to the top of the sweeping staircase, and his frustration with his stubborn, insubordinate pilot changed to white-hot desire as he watched her walk gracefully down the stairs. The dress was a Luca De Rossi creation, an elegant floor-length sheath of silk the colour of a summer sky that matched exactly the blue of Lexi's eyes. Her pale gold hair had been left loose and fell past her shoulders like a silken curtain, framing a face as beautiful and serene as a Raphael virgin.

Kadir was aware of every painful beat of his heart as he strode across the hall.

'Am I late?' Lexi gave him a rueful look. 'I couldn't reach the zip on my dress.'

'Why didn't you call one of the maids to assist you?'

She shrugged. 'It didn't occur to me to ask for help. I made a hook out of a coat hanger and managed to pull the zip up with it. I served in the armed forces for ten years and I'm used to working out solutions to problems,' she reminded Kadir.

'Did you often wear evening gowns in Afghanistan?' He did not know whether to be exasperated or amused by her fierce independence.

'Of course not…' She hesitated. 'I've never worn a House of De Rossi dress before, or any other designer dress, for that matter. It's beautiful, and obviously I will pay for it.'

'Fortunately, we have been called in to dinner,' he murmured, offering her his arm, 'so we'll have to save the argument until later.'

'We don't need to argue. You simply have to accept that I won't allow you to pay for my clothes.'

His eyes glittered. 'You always have to have the last word. Stubbornness is not an attractive quality in a woman.'

Lexi flashed him a cool smile that made Kadir grind his teeth. 'I'm not hoping to attract you, Your Highness. Unlike just about every other woman here tonight,' she added drily.

When she had first caught sight of him, dressed in a white tuxedo that looked stunning against his olive-gold skin, she had been blown away by his good looks and smouldering sensuality, and a glance around the room revealed that she was not the only woman who could not take her eyes off him.

They had reached the dining room, and Kadir held out a chair for Lexi to sit down. He was aware of the subtle and, in some cases, not so subtle glances directed at him from the other female party guests. Lexi was the only woman he wanted, but he could not tell her and he could not allow their mutual attraction to ignite. However, as she sat down, he was compelled by a force beyond his control to lower his head so that he could inhale the evocative scent of her perfume.

Lexi was suddenly conscious that Kadir had leaned closer to her and his face was almost touching hers. She held her breath as the close-trimmed stubble on his jaw scraped against her cheek, and only released it when he lifted his head and moved to sit down on the chair beside her. She took a sip of water and waited for her racing pulse to slow before she dared to look at him. His lazy smile did peculiar things to her insides. She wished she had not come down to dinner. She felt so tense that the thought of putting food into her stomach made her shudder. It had only been the thought that he was very likely to come to her room and force her to obey him that had persuaded her to put on the dress that she had discovered wrapped in tissue on the bed.

Heat stained Lexi's cheeks as it occurred to her that she had never in her life allowed a man to force her to do anything she did not want to do. And why did the idea of being made to obey Kadir conjure shockingly erotic images in her mind? What was happening to her? she wondered grimly. Tomorrow she would be going to Zenhab. Pulling out was not an option; she could not afford to pay the penalty clause in her contract. But, more than that, it was a matter of pride that she learned to deal with His Royal Hotness and prove that she had not been fazed when he had kissed her in the pool in Monaco.

Kadir was charming and entertaining during dinner, but it was his unexpected gentleness when he spoke to the over-eager Danielle that surprised Lexi. His charisma and sexual magnetism she could handle, just, she thought ruefully. But the discovery that he could be kind and, dare she even think it, sensitive, was an element to him she had been unaware of until now. Heavens, if he carried on being Mr Nice Guy she might even grow to like him!

'I understand you are a helicopter pilot and flew rescue missions in Afghanistan.' Chuck Weinberg's strong Texan drawl dragged Lexi from her thoughts. 'Is your father a military man?'

'My father...' Lexi's hesitation fired Kadir's curiosity. "He's a doctor. Actually, both my parents are in the medical profession; my father is a heart surgeon and my mother is a neurologist.'

'They must be clever people! It's curious that you didn't inherit an interest in medicine from your parents,' Chuck commented.

God knew what genes she had inherited from her biological parents, Lexi thought bleakly. Her mother had provided sexual favours for a living, and her father had been one of Cathy's clients. The man whose blood ran through her veins was nameless, faceless, and the knowledge that she would never know his identity made her feel incomplete.

After dinner the party moved into the orangerie, where there was dancing to a five-piece jazz band. Lexi withdrew to an alcove and watched Kadir work his way around the room. No female between the ages of eighteen and eighty was safe from his magnetic charm, she thought as he finished dancing with Danielle Weinberg and swept a white-haired lady onto the dance floor.

'I should have expected Kadir would try to seduce my grandmother, and that Nonna Violetta would adore him.'

Lexi glanced at Luca De Rossi, who had come to stand beside her. 'He's certainly the life and soul of the party,' she said drily.

An amused smile crossed Luca's handsome face. Similar in height and build to Kadir, he possessed film star looks, with jet-black hair, classically sculpted features and an air of polished sophistication that marked him out as a European aristocrat.

'Don't be fooled by Kadir's playboy image,' Luca murmured. 'He plays hard but he works harder and he is prepared to devote his life to Zenhab.'

Lexi restrained herself from asking what kind of work the Prince of Pleasure had ever done. 'I understand you became friends with Kadir at Eton? Did you also know Charles Fairfax at school?'

'He was in the year below Kadir and I.' The Italian shrugged an elegant shoulder. 'I can't say Charlie was a close friend. Why do you ask?'

'He's going to marry my sister.'

Luca looked surprised. 'How curious,' he murmured.

Lexi wanted to ask him what he meant, but her thoughts scattered as Kadir appeared at her side. 'You have monopolised my pilot for long enough,' he told Luca lightly, but beneath his easy tone was a possessiveness that made Lexi bristle. 'Dance with me,' he commanded.

She shook her head. 'I can't dance, and you are hardly short of partners. Every woman in the room is hoping it'll be her turn next to be swept onto the dance floor by the Arabian version of Fred Astaire.'

Kadir laughed softly as he clamped his hands on her waist and whisked her around the room. 'There's no need for you to be jealous. I only have eyes for you, angel face.'

'I am *not* jealous!' She knew he was teasing her, playing a familiar game that he had played all the past week, so why was her heart thudding painfully fast beneath her ribs? She brought the tip of her stiletto heel down on his toe and gave him a look of wide-eyed innocence. 'Oops. I warned you I can't dance.'

His eyes glittered with an unspoken challenge that sent a frisson of excitement down

Lexi's spine. 'Be careful, or I might be tempted to expose your secret right here while we are dancing in front of all these people.'

'What secret…?' She snatched a sharp breath, remembering how he had kissed her in the swimming pool and she had arched her body towards him in an unmistakable offer that had revealed her desire. The memory of that kiss made Lexi feel vulnerable and exposed—to him. The hunger in Kadir's eyes—no trace of teasing now—caused molten heat to flood through her veins.

Confused by her reaction to a man she knew to be a playboy, she stumbled and Kadir immediately tightened his arms around her, drawing her closer so that her hips came into searing contact with his. The hard ridge of his arousal pushed against her pelvis. She did not dare meet his gaze but she knew from the harsh sound of his breathing that he was in as much danger of bursting into flames as she was.

Why him? she asked herself bitterly. Why had she never felt this intensity of need, this overpowering desire for any other man, including the man she had planned to marry? She had never come close to losing control with Steven. Until she had met Kadir she hadn't known what it was like to ache in every part of her body, or for her breasts to feel heavy and her nipples hot and hard, so that she knew without glancing down that they were visibly outlined beneath her silk dress.

'Excuse me…' She did not care that the tremor in her voice betrayed her tension as she pulled out of his arms and walked swiftly across the dance floor. She was simply desperate to regain control of her wayward body and wanton thoughts.

Kadir watched Lexi's slender figure weave through the other dancers, and it took every bit of his will power not to go after her, sweep her up into his arms and carry her off to—where? he asked himself derisively. Taking her to bed was not an option. It had to end now, this madness, the longing for something he could not have—and quite possibly he wanted all the more because Lexi was off-limits.

He saw Chuck Weinberg beckoning to him from the library, where they had arranged to discuss the business deal that would be hugely beneficial to Zenhab. His last night of freedom ended here, Kadir told himself as he strode towards the library.

Lexi checked her watch and saw that it was past midnight. The party was winding down and the guests were leaving. She was due to fly the helicopter to Milan Airport in the morning so that it could be loaded onto a transporter plane for the journey to Zenhab. It would be an early start to what promised to be a long day and she knew she should go to bed, but she had never felt less like sleeping in her life.

She wondered where Kadir was. He had disappeared from the party a couple of hours ago and Lexi had not seen him, or the attractive redhead who was almost wearing a daringly low-cut dress, since. He was not her responsibility, she reminded herself. She was employed as his pilot and his personal life was none of her business.

Hadn't he made it his business when he had kissed her? whispered a voice inside her head. She frowned. The kiss had meant nothing to him. He had been playing with her like he had done all week, but tonight he had obviously grown bored of the game and turned his attention to the well-endowed redhead.

Feeling restless and refusing to admit that Kadir was the cause, she stepped outside onto the long terrace that ran along the back of the house. The Villa De Rossi's magnificent formal gardens were dappled in silver moonlight but, as Lexi slipped like a shadow along the path leading down to the lake, the moon was partially obscured by clouds racing across the sky. She drew her pashmina tighter around her shoulders. Autumn in northern Italy was much warmer than in England but, as she stood at the edge of the lake, raindrops began to bounce onto the surface, falling faster and faster until the water seemed to dance.

A wooden summer house further along the path was the only place to shelter from the rain shower, and luckily she found the door was unlocked. Inky darkness greeted her as she stepped inside and an even darker voice demanded, 'What do you want?'

'*Kadir?*' Lexi's yelp of fright turned to shock and her heart leapt into her throat as a faint yellow light filled the cabin and she saw that Kadir had lit a gas lamp on the wall. 'What are you doing here?' Her eyes flew to an old sofa piled with cushions and realisation dawned. She guessed the redhead was hiding somewhere. 'I'm sorry if I've interrupted something.'

His heavy brows drew together. 'What do you mean?'

'I assume you are here with someone.'

'By *someone* I suppose you mean a woman?' Kadir growled. 'Why do you always jump to the worst conclusion based on rubbish the paparazzi have written about me in the past?'

Lexi flushed as it became apparent that there was no one else in the summer house. 'What was I supposed to think? Why were you sitting here in the dark?'

He shrugged. 'I went for a stroll because I needed some air and ended up at the summer house. I used to come here with Luca when we were teenagers; I stayed with him sometimes during the school holidays. He taught me to sail on the lake.'

They had been halcyon days, Kadir brooded, before his father had suffered the stroke that had left him paralysed and unable to rule, before his uncle Jamal had seized power, and before he had been forced to agree to an arranged marriage in a bid to maintain peace and stability in Zenhab.

Lexi glanced out of the window. Through the darkness, the twinkling lights of the villages strung around the shores of Lake Como revealed the vast size of the lake. 'I imagine sailing is popular on the lake.' She remembered that he had skippered the Zenhabian team that had won the America's Cup. 'Why did you decide to take up offshore sailing?'

'There are no lakes in Zenhab,' he said drily. 'Away from the coast, most of the land is desert and rock. How do you feel about returning to a desert environment?'

'I'm interested to see a new country and, unlike Afghanistan, there isn't a war in Zenhab so I might get a chance to see the beauty of a desert landscape without having to worry about avoiding landmines.'

Kadir exhaled heavily. His father had ended the civil war in Zenhab and established peace between the tribes two decades ago. With his last breath Sultan Khalif had begged his son to maintain unity in the kingdom. Kadir had vowed to carry out his father's wish, for it was his wish too. He loved the kingdom that he had been destined from birth to rule. It was a small sacrifice to give up his right to fall in love and marry a woman of his choice. Perhaps it was even a blessing. He had learned from his parents that love was a precarious base for marriage. His father had been broken-hearted when Kadir's mother had returned to England for good.

Lust, on the other hand, was easy to understand. It was nothing more than chemistry, and it was a bitter irony, Kadir mused, that the chemical reaction between him and Lexi was blistering.

In the semi-dark summer house he was so aware of her that every skin cell on his body tingled, and he could feel the thunderous drumbeat of his desire pounding in his veins. He had never met anyone like her before, never admired any woman as much as he admired

Lexi. She was beautiful, brave, intensely annoying, utterly intriguing—his brain told him to move away from her, but his body wasn't listening. His eyes locked with hers and his heart flipped a somersault when he saw that fire had replaced the ice in her bright blue gaze.

Was it so wrong to want to taste her one last time? To capture a memory that must last him a lifetime. *One kiss*... He lowered his head and watched her pupils darken, heard the soft catch of her breath as he grazed his lips across hers and felt them tremble and open like the velvet-soft petals of an English rose.

One kiss, he assured himself.

She was sweetness and fire, his delight and quite possibly his destruction. When he had kissed her in the swimming pool he had not dared allow their bodies to come into contact, but now she melted into him, soft and pliant against his hard musculature. With a groan, he wrapped one arm around her waist and threaded his other hand into her long silky hair. Her perfume—a blend of crisp citrus and sweet jasmine—so appropriate for her, he thought—wrapped around him and he closed his eyes and sought her mouth blindly, his other senses, of touch and taste, heightened so that the feel of her lips beneath his was beyond pleasure.

The first time Kadir had kissed her in Monaco, Lexi knew that his intention had been to prove a point and show her that he was in control. She had understood that he had been angry because she had challenged him. But there was no anger now. They had not been having one of their verbal sparring matches and, rather than trying to show her who was boss, Kadir seemed to have seduction in his mind. His lips were firm on hers and he kissed her with demanding hunger, yet there was an unexpected tenderness in his passion that answered a need deep within her. The bold thrust of his tongue into her mouth shattered her resistance and destroyed the mental barriers she *always* kept in place.

She could not control the tremor that ran through her as he trailed his lips over her cheek, her throat, and found the pulse beating frantically at its base. Distracted by him sliding the strap of her dress over her shoulder, she felt something hard at the back of her knees and belatedly realised it was the sofa.

He eased her down onto the cushions and knelt above her. The fierce glitter in his eyes was a promise and a warning of his intent. Lexi held her breath as he slipped his hands beneath her and ran her zip far enough down her spine to allow him to peel away the top of her dress. The air felt cool on her breasts; his palms felt warm on her bare flesh. Glancing down, the sight of his darkly tanned hands on her creamy pale breasts was incredibly erotic, and when he rubbed his thumb pads across her tender nipples the sensation was so exquisite that she could not restrain a soft moan.

'You are more beautiful even than I imagined.' His voice, roughened with desire, broke the intense silence of the dimly lit cabin.

Reality pushed, unwelcome, into Lexi's thoughts. She wasn't a novice when it came to sex; she was an independent woman, free to do as she pleased. She could no longer deny that she wanted to make love with Kadir, but choice also meant taking responsibility for herself. 'I'm not on the Pill,' she murmured. 'Do you have anything with you?'

Lexi's words were as effective as a cold shower. Once again Kadir acknowledged the irony of bad timing. If she had asked him the same question six months ago he would have been able to assure her that he always carried condoms with him. But he had made a commitment to himself to end the playboy lifestyle, in preparation for his marriage.

His desire for Lexi was blazing out of control, but in his heart burned the need to prove to himself that he was an honourable man like his father had been, a man fit to be Sultan of Zenhab and fulfil the destiny of a desert king.

Ignoring the painful throb of his arousal, he got up from the sofa and tugged Lexi's dress back over her breasts. She caught her breath as the silk grazed her nipples, and the evidence of how sensitive her breasts were almost shattered Kadir's resolve to end what he should never have begun.

'We must go back to the house,' he said abruptly as he thrust her pashmina into her hands, and felt relieved when she wrapped it around her so that he could no longer see the hard points of her nipples jutting beneath her dress.

'Shouldn't we wait until it stops raining?' Lexi hesitated when Kadir opened the cabin door and she saw the torrential downpour. But he had already stepped onto the porch. He slid out of his jacket and draped it around her shoulders before he grabbed her hand and practically dragged her along the path.

'We need to go back now.'

His urgency filled Lexi with anticipation. In the cabin she had been aware of his hunger, the need for sexual fulfilment that had almost overwhelmed both of them. But safe sex could not be ignored and Kadir was clearly impatient to take her to his bedroom, where presumably he had contraceptives and they could make love with peace of mind.

Was she out of her mind? demanded a voice inside her head. It defied common sense to sleep with a playboy. But she was tired of being sensible. Her job as a helicopter pilot in the RAF and then with the coastguard agency had required her to take risks, but on a personal level she had played it safe for far too long. Why shouldn't she enjoy everything the Prince of Pleasure had to offer?

Lexi's heart was thumping as Kadir ushered her into the villa through a side door and up a back staircase used by the servants to the third floor, where the guest bedrooms were.

Her smile faltered and she gave him a puzzled look when he stopped in the corridor outside her bedroom and said brusquely, 'Goodnight.'

Goodnight! 'I…I don't understand. I thought…'

The memory of his barely restrained passion ten minutes earlier made her abandon her usual diffidence. She ached for him and she had been certain that he wanted her with the same white-hot need. His chiselled features gave no clue to his thoughts and some of Lexi's certainty faded as she stared into his eyes that were the colour of dark umber, without the teasing glint she was used to seeing. 'I assumed we were going to spend the night together,' she said huskily.

In his wilder days Kadir had slept with more women than he could remember, but he had never felt as much of a bastard as he did now for not sleeping with Lexi. The irony would be laughable if he felt like laughing, but he doubted that he would ever laugh again. There was no good way to handle the situation and only one thing he could say.

'I'm sorry. I should not have let things get out of hand the way they did.'

Lexi's racing heart juddered to a standstill. Oh, no, not sorry, she thought bitterly. Let him be mocking, sarcastic—anything but pitying. She heard Steven's voice inside her head.

I'm sorry, Lexi. I shouldn't have allowed our relationship to develop when I knew that my girlfriend and baby were waiting for me back in England. It felt like you and I were in another world in Afghanistan. But the truth is that I'm not free to marry you because I already have a family.

Rejection was hurtful and humiliating. After Steven had dumped her she had vowed never to put herself in such a vulnerable position again.

So what was she doing hovering outside her

bedroom in the vain hope that Kadir might change his mind and take her to bed? *How much more vulnerable could she feel?* Kadir had been playing games with her ever since they'd met, Lexi thought grimly.

'Good manners prevent me from telling you what you can do with your apology,' she said, her voice so tightly wound that it shook with the strain of retaining her last dregs of pride. She opened her bedroom door and gave a cynical laugh. 'I should thank you for stopping me from making the worst mistake of my life.' Something in his darkly beautiful face made her insides twist. 'Everything is a game to you, isn't it?'

'*Damn it*, Lexi. Of course I don't think this is a game.'

To Lexi's astonishment, Kadir drove his clenched fist against the door frame, and it was a testament to the solidity of the wood that it did not splinter beneath the powerful blow. 'The situation is complicated,' he said savagely. 'I want to spend the night with you and make love to you. But I am not free to do what I want.'

'But…you are a Sultan. You can do whatever you like.'

'I wish that were true.'

Lexi felt a curious sense of déjà vu. Steven

had admitted that he wasn't free to be with her because he had a long-term partner and a child. She lifted her chin and stared into Kadir's eyes. 'Why are you not free?'

An indefinable emotion flickered in his dark gaze. 'I am betrothed to the princess of the mountain tribes in Zenhab.'

'You're engaged to be *married*?' Her shock rapidly turned to anger. 'Then what the hell were you doing coming on to me when presumably you are in love with your fiancée— you...cheating *louse*?'

A nerve jumped in Kadir's cheek. 'I am not a cheat. Nor am I in love with Princess Haleema. I've never even met her.' He saw the confusion in Lexi's eyes and his tone softened. 'We are not engaged as you would understand the word. A marriage arrangement was made by our families, and I had to agree to it to keep peace in Zenhab. After his stroke, my father was convinced that the marriage would forge stronger ties with the mountain tribes and ensure stability in the kingdom that had once been torn apart by civil war.'

Lexi stared at him. The story of an arranged marriage sounded convenient, but she sensed that Kadir was telling her the truth. 'I didn't realise that arranged marriages took place in Zenhab.'

'*Forced* marriages will not be allowed under the new law I have introduced. And in fact they are rare. Many families believe in arranged marriages where sons and daughters are introduced to a potential spouse, but marriage can only take place if it is the choice of the bride and groom.'

'Did you have a choice about becoming engaged to the princess?'

'No,' Kadir said heavily. Agreeing to marry Haleema had been the only way he could claim the Crown—his birthright—from his uncle. 'It was my father's dying wish that I should ensure the future stability and safety of our country. Haleema was only a child at that time, but I gave my father my word that I would honour my promise and take her as my bride when she was old enough to marry. When I return to Zenhab I intend to fulfil my duty.'

Lexi guessed it was a duty that weighed heavy on Kadir's shoulders. She remembered Luca De Rossi had said that Kadir was prepared to devote his life to his kingdom and she felt a grudging respect for his determination to honour the promise he had made as a young man. But he had not treated her honourably, she thought with a flash of anger.

'You should have been honest with me from the start. You had no right to…to flirt with

me.' She felt sick when she remembered his
sexy smile and the gleam of sensual promise
in his eyes. The realisation that it had all been
a game to him was humiliating. Just like Steven, Kadir had not considered her feelings,
she thought painfully. He had kissed her and
started to make love to her, knowing that he
was promised to another woman. To both men,
she had been unimportant, and the realisation
opened up the raw feelings of rejection that
had haunted her for years.

'I know it was wrong of me to kiss you,'
Kadir growled. 'I cannot deny that I desire
you. From the moment we met, we were drawn
to each other.' He held her gaze and dared her
to deny it. 'But I give you my word that I won't
kiss you again, and when we are in Zenhab I
will treat you with courtesy and respect.'

'I can't go to Zenhab with you now! How
can we forget what nearly happened between
us tonight?'

'We have to forget,' Kadir said harshly. 'I
still need a helicopter pilot.'

'You could release me from my contract and
employ another pilot.'

He shook his head. 'I chose you especially
because one of your duties will be to fly Haleema between her home in the mountains and
the palace. Her family are very traditional and

she will only be permitted to travel with a female pilot.'

'You want me to chaperone your fiancée?' Lexi was tempted to tell him what he could do with his damned job, but hot on the heels of her temper was the realisation that she still had to repay her mother's debts and she could not afford the financial penalty if she broke her contract with Kadir. It was also a question of pride. Kadir had guessed that she found him attractive, but if he could forget their passion that had almost blazed out of control in the summer house then so could she.

She stepped into her bedroom and forced her lips into a dismissive smile. 'Fine, I'll come to Zenhab as per our agreement,' she told him coolly. 'I'm sure I'll have no problem forgetting the regrettable incident that took place tonight, and from now on I will expect our relationship to be purely professional, Your Highness.'

she will only be permitted to have, with a human pilot.

You will need to phone Lexi through to us with his request ...
of her current job, but before she, she had to repay her mother's debts and she could
would then distributed responsibly she back that

CHAPTER SEVEN

LEXI STARED OUT of the plane window at the seemingly unending expanse of saffron-coloured sand that had been wind-whipped into towering dunes and sinuous ridges which resembled a giant serpent writhing across the land. In the far distance she could see craggy grey mountains, beyond which, according to her guidebook, lay Zenhab's wild and barren northern lands where a few ancient Bedouin tribes lived.

Looking in the other direction, she saw the outlines of modern skyscrapers alongside elegant minarets and curving mosque roofs. Zenhab's position in the Arabian Sea made it an important trading route, and its rich cultural history and architecture reflected the periods in time when the country had been under Portuguese and, later, Persian rule.

As the plane flew over the capital city, Mezeira, Kadir's chief adviser, Yusuf bin Hilal, pointed out places of interest. 'There is the royal palace. You see how the pure white walls sparkle in the sunshine as though the stones are mixed with diamonds? They are not, of course,' Yusuf explained. 'The bricks contain a special kind of sand that gives the jewel effect.'

'It looks like a fairy tale palace from *Arabian Nights* with all those towers and spires. It reminds me a little of the Taj Mahal in India.'

'The people of Zenhab believe that *our* Sultan's royal palace is the most beautiful building in the world,' Yusuf said proudly.

'I understand that in the past there was unrest in the mountain territories of Zenhab,' Lexi commented.

Yusuf nodded. 'There was a terrible civil war. But the present Sultan's father, Sultan Khalif, established peace in the kingdom and for the past decade his son has introduced a programme of liberalisation and modernisation that has resulted in economic growth for the country. Sultan Kadir works tirelessly to attract foreign business and investment to Zenhab and he is regarded by the majority of the population as an inspired leader.'

Yusuf pointed to another building. 'That is Zenhab's first university, opened by Sultan Kadir five years ago and partly funded by him personally. His advancement of education for rich and poor alike, and especially for women, has gained him much support, and sadly a few enemies. The Sultan has received death threats, but he still insists on walking among his people whenever he can. He is a truly great man,' Yusuf said reverently.

Every member of Kadir's staff that Lexi had spoken to seemed to share Yusuf's opinion. Her own opinion of him as a playboy prince was changing since she had discovered that he was willing to sacrifice his right to choose a wife and had agreed to an arranged marriage because he believed it was best for his kingdom. She respected his determination to put his duty to his country above his personal desires, and she knew she should be grateful to him for being honest with her in Italy instead of taking her to bed. But she had lied when she'd told him that she would easily forget the passionate moments they had shared in the summer house. He dominated her thoughts, day and night, but now that they had arrived in Zenhab he would soon marry his Princess, she thought dully.

She had not seen Kadir since they had boarded the plane and he had walked past his entourage of staff in the main cabin on his way to his private suite at the front. Once the plane had landed, she'd expected him to reappear, but there was no sign of him as she'd followed Yusuf down the steps and onto the tarmac. To her surprise, the members of Kadir's staff who had travelled abroad with him stood with the plane's crew, forming what appeared to be a reception committee, and Lexi had no option but to stand in line with them. 'What's happening?' she whispered to Yusuf.

'By tradition, when the Sultan returns home, glorious from his conquests and battles abroad, although, of course, he has business meetings now rather than battles,' the adviser hastily explained, 'he is escorted through the streets of the city to the palace by horsemen.'

Yusuf's voice was drowned out by the sound of thundering hooves and Lexi turned to see a great dust cloud, through which appeared thirty or so horsemen wearing traditional Zenhabian clothes—white robes with brightly coloured short-sleeved jackets on top and white headdresses which billowed behind them as the horsemen raced along the runway.

Glancing up at the plane, Lexi's heart lurched as Kadir appeared in the doorway and stood on the top step. Like the horsemen, he was dressed in a white robe, and his jacket was exquisitely embroidered in red and gold. At his waist he wore a wide leather belt and a terrifying-looking ceremonial knife in a jewelled holder. His white headdress, which Lexi knew was called a *keffiyeh*, was held in place by a circle of black and gold rope. He looked regal and remote, the powerful ruler of his desert kingdom, and far removed from his alterego of an English Earl.

Even from the distance that separated Lexi from him, she could see the dark brilliance of his eyes. She could not stop herself from staring at him, riveted by his handsome face, and she felt the same curious ache in her heart that she had felt in Italy when he had admitted that he was not free to make love to her.

He descended the steps and walked past the line of staff. Lexi found she was holding her breath as he came closer. She willed him to turn his head and notice her, but he strode straight past, leaving in his wake the spicy tang of his cologne that hung in the hot, still air and teased her senses.

She closed her eyes, assailed by memories of when he had kissed her in the summer house at Lake Como. She remembered the heat of his body through his silk shirt, the feel of his hands on her skin when he had pulled her dress down and caressed her breasts. Frantically, she tried to block out the erotic images in her mind as she reminded herself that Kadir should not have kissed her because he was engaged to another woman. She felt as if a knife had sliced through her heart, and she swayed on her feet.

'Miss Howard?' Yusuf sounded anxious. 'Are you going to faint? The heat of the desert can take some getting used to, especially for someone as fair-skinned and delicate-looking as yourself,' the adviser murmured sympathetically.

Lexi's eyes snapped open. 'I assure you I am not in the least delicate,' she told Yusuf tersely. She was furious with herself for reacting to Kadir the way she had. It could not happen again. She was not a silly lovestruck girl, wilting beneath the desert sun and a surfeit of hormones. She had come to Zenhab to do a job and she *must* forget those passionate moments she had spent in the Sultan's arms, as it appeared that he had forgotten her.

Kadir had reached the group of horsemen and a huge black horse was brought to him. He swung himself into the saddle and reached behind his shoulder to withdraw a long curved sword from a jewelled scabbard that Lexi saw hanging down his back. The horsemen did likewise, and held their swords aloft, the steel blades glinting in the fierce sun as their Sultan gave a loud victory cry.

The scene could have taken place centuries ago, when the great Islamic leader Saladin had fought the English King Richard in the Crusades, Lexi thought. This was the real Kadir Al Sulaimar, she realised. There was no sign of the charismatic playboy she had met when they had been in Europe. The Sultan of Zenhab looked stern and forbidding, yet she could not forget how his mouth had felt on hers when he had kissed her, his unexpected tenderness as he had teased her lips apart and explored her with his tongue.

Her breath caught in her throat as Kadir turned his head and stared directly at her. Lexi had the strange sense that he was remembering the moments when they had fallen into each other's arms in the summer house. But the gleam in his eyes must have been sunlight reflected off his sword. He turned away and gave a blood-curdling cry before he galloped his horse down the runway, pursued by the thirty horsemen, in a cloud of dust and flashing horses' hooves and white *keffiyeh's* streaming behind the cavalcade.

She could not ask for a better place to work, Lexi conceded a few days later. She had been given a luxurious apartment at the palace with her own private terrace and pool, and she had access to the beautiful royal gardens, where it was pleasant to sit by the ornamental fountains and feel the cool spray on her face.

Kadir had a busy schedule and attended meetings and functions most days, requiring Lexi to fly him by helicopter to towns across the kingdom. The previous day she had flown him along Zenhab's stunning coast so that he could inspect the site of a new hotel complex, which his adviser Yusuf had said was going to be built by the Russian businessman Boris Denisov.

Apart from bidding her good morning, Kadir had not spoken to her, and he'd sat in the rear of the helicopter. He obviously intended to keep their relationship strictly professional, but Lexi had been aware of his brooding gaze burning between her shoulder blades during the flight.

She was lonely at the palace, and missed the sense of camaraderie she'd had with her friends in the coastguard agency and the RAF. From one of the tallest towers she was able to look out over the desert, and remembering the dusty military base at Camp Bastion in Afghanistan and the other pilots she had flown missions with increased her sense of isolation.

As was her habit, she turned to physical exercise to relieve her frustration, and went running every morning before the sun rose high in the sky and the temperature soared. She'd also discovered an air-conditioned gym in the palace where Kadir's bodyguards worked out. Ashar and Nasim were reasonably fluent in English, and Lexi spoke some Arabic. Once they had got over their initial hesitancy at sharing the gym with a woman, the two young men were friendly and their company went some way to alleviating her loneliness.

'I'll grant you that men are physically stronger than women, but in a test of stamina and endurance women can equal, or even beat their male counterparts,' Lexi argued one afternoon.

Nasim stepped off the treadmill. 'Okay, prove it. Push-ups until one of us gives up.'

Determination gleamed in Lexi's eyes. 'You're on. Ashar, you can act as judge.'

Kadir frowned as he walked down the corridor to the gym and heard voices from behind the door. He had been busy with matters of state since he had returned to the palace, and this was his first chance for a workout. He had hoped to find the gym empty but, as he opened the door, he came to an abrupt halt at the sight of one of his bodyguards and his private pilot stretched out on gym mats, pumping their bodies up and down in a series of push-ups.

From where he was standing he had a perfect view of Lexi's pert bottom covered in bright pink satin shorts—lifting and lowering, lifting and lowering in a steady rhythm that had a predictable effect on his pulse rate. He visualised her slender body arched above him, the tips of her bare breasts brushing his chest as she slowly lowered herself onto him… His arousal was instant and so hard that he hastily held his towel in front of him and cursed beneath his breath.

'What is going on?' He knew it was a stupid question, but the sound of his voice had the desired effect of making Lexi and the bodyguard stop what they were doing and jump to their feet. The guilty expression on Nasim's face heightened Kadir's anger. Why did the bodyguard look guilty, unless the push-ups were a prelude to another form of exercise? he thought grimly.

'Do you not kneel before your Sultan?' he demanded to Nasim and Ashar.

'Your Majesty!' The men immediately dropped down onto one knee, but Lexi remained standing and met Kadir's hard stare with a challenge in her eyes as she placed her hands on her hips.

'Is there a problem, Your Highness?'

You're damned right there's a problem, Kadir thought to himself. But he was not going to admit that his body felt as if it was about to

explode, or that he was unbearably tempted to
dismiss the bodyguards and make love to his
feisty helicopter pilot right there on the gym
mat. He was shocked and, if he was honest,
ashamed of his ferocious desire for Lexi. No
other woman had ever made him feel so out
of control. He was a powerful Sultan, but she
reminded him that he was also just a man with
an inexplicable hunger clawing in his gut.

'My bodyguards owe you an apology. They
should have respected your privacy and de-
parted from the gym while you were exercis-
ing.'

Lexi shrugged. 'They offered to leave, but
I don't have a problem with them being here.
I was used to training alongside men when I
was in the RAF.'

Kadir's jaw tightened. 'You must understand
that we have different ways here than in England.'

Lexi knew that although Zenhab was one of
the more liberal countries in the Middle East,
there were rules regarding men and women so-
cialising together. 'I understand that I wouldn't
be allowed to mix with men in a public gym,
but this is a private facility and surely the same
rules don't apply? After all, the palace is your
home, and you make the rules.'

'That's right,' Kadir said in a dangerously

soft voice intended to warn Lexi that she was close to overstepping the mark, 'and my rule is that from now on you will be allocated separate times to use the gym when the men are not allowed in.'

Lexi could see that further arguing would be pointless. The Sultan had spoken. She glanced at the bodyguards, who were still kneeling, their heads bowed. Usually Kadir had an easygoing relationship with his protection officers and she did not understand why he was so annoyed. She did not want to lose her friendship with the two bodyguards. They were her only companions at the palace and if she was banned from spending time with them she knew she would feel even more isolated.

'Please don't blame Nasim and Ashar. It was my fault if any rules were broken.'

Her defence of the two men further fuelled Kadir's temper. He held the door open for Lexi to leave. 'I will deal with them as I see fit, before I deal with you.'

'*Deal* with me?' The vague threat was like a red rag to a bull. 'What are you going to do, send me to bed with no tea? Put me across your knee?'

'Would you like me to spank you?' Kadir murmured dulcetly. He had followed Lexi out into the corridor so that the bodyguards could not hear their conversation.

A shockingly erotic image of him holding her face down over his thighs while he chastised her flashed into her mind and fiery colour flooded her cheeks. 'Of course not,' she said sharply.

His husky chuckle warned her that he had read her thoughts, and Lexi's embarrassment became more acute. But she wondered why he was clutching his towel in front of his hips as if his life depended on it. Her senses, acutely attuned to him, detected the undefinable essence of male pheromones, the scent of sexual arousal.

'Why does it matter to you if I hang out with Nasim and Ashar in my free time?' she burst out. 'There is no one else I can socialise with and I realise that it is not possible for me to go out in the city in the evenings on my own. I feel like I'm trapped at the palace.'

'You have been provided with excellent accommodation and leisure facilities; I did not realise you expected to have a full social calendar. The palace is hardly a prison,' Kadir said drily.

Lexi gave up trying to make him understand that she craved the company of other people. When she had served in the RAF she'd had a wide group of friends and had felt a sense of belonging that had been missing with her adoptive parents. Being alone gave her too much time to think, and stirred up her old feelings of loneliness and inadequacy she had felt as a child.

But Kadir knew nothing about her troubled background, and she had no intention of telling him. A dignified retreat seemed her best option but, as usual, she was determined to have the last word.

'Perhaps hard physical exertion in the gym will relieve some of your tension,' she murmured, before she turned and marched down the corridor, leaving Kadir fighting the temptation to go after her and kiss her sassy mouth into submission. There was only one kind of physical exertion that he knew was guaranteed to relieve his sexual frustration, but he could not make love to Lexi, no matter how much he wanted to.

Lexi had hoped that a punishing fifteen-kilometre run through the palace grounds would expend her anger with Kadir for criticising her friendship with his bodyguards. But when she returned to her apartment her temper was still simmering, and to cool down she dived into the pool and swam twenty lengths. Breathless at last, she hauled herself onto the poolside and shook her wet hair back from her face.

She stiffened when she saw Kadir was standing watching her. 'I assume you have no objection to me swimming in my private pool?' She hoped her cool tone disguised the heat that surged through her as she drank in the sight of him in cream chinos and a black polo shirt. His eyes were hidden behind designer shades and he was so outrageously attractive that Lexi almost jumped back into the pool to hide her body's reaction to him. Her nipples were as hard as pebbles and she hastily dragged the towel around her shoulders to hide her traitorous body from view.

He gave her a lazy smile, no hint now of his earlier bad mood. 'None at all,' he assured her, 'although I am wondering why you aren't wearing your silver bikini.'

She shrugged. 'A one-piece is more comfortable for swimming. But another reason is that I *do* appreciate the cultural differences in the Middle East. Although the pool is for my private use, the palace staff are around and out of respect for them I chose to wear a swimming costume. It's more demure than a bikini.'

Demure! Kadir wondered if Lexi had any idea how sexy she looked in her sleek navy costume, which clung to every dip and curve of her superbly toned figure. He could not forget the image of her taut buttocks covered in tight pink shorts pumping up and down when she had been doing push-ups in the gym. Fire heated his blood and he altered his position to hide the evidence of his arousal beneath his trousers, which suddenly felt uncomfortably tight.

'Anyway, there is no point in me wearing my bikini when I'm not allowed to socialise with anyone at the palace, or get a chance to meet a guy who I would like to untie the strings,' Lexi said defiantly.

Kadir's eyes narrowed. 'Always you challenge me, Lexi. You want to be careful that I do not rise to your bait.'

Her gaze did not waver from his. 'You have already demonstrated that that isn't going to happen. I made a fool of myself in Italy,' she said bitterly. She hated herself for the way she had responded to him like a gauche teenager on a first date. He was the only man who had ever made her lose control and the level of her desire had shocked and shamed her.

She suddenly became conscious of how close they were standing. The air between them throbbed with tension and every nerve ending on her body tingled with sexual awareness that she knew he felt too.

'I was the fool, for kissing you when I knew I was not free to make love to you,' Kadir said harshly. He picked up her robe and handed it to her. 'Put this on, before I forget my good intentions.' He gave a wry smile that did not reach his eyes, and Lexi had a sudden sense of how lonely his role as Sultan must be. His father was dead, his mother lived abroad and he was destined to marry a woman he had never met who had been chosen for him.

If he had not been contracted to his arranged marriage, she knew that they would be lovers by now. His desire for her smouldered in his dark eyes, but the firm set of his jaw told her that he would put his duty to his kingdom before his personal desires.

She pulled on the robe and tied the belt tightly around her waist. 'Why did you want to see me?'

Because he could not keep away from her, Kadir thought grimly. She was like a drug in his veins and even the knowledge that his desire for her was forbidden did not stop him thinking about her constantly.

'I came to apologise for my behaviour earlier. I appreciate that you might feel cut off from your friends and family. I have come with an invitation to tea from someone who I believe you could become friends with.'

Lexi eyed him suspiciously. 'Who?'

His grin made him look suddenly younger. 'I'm taking you to meet the most important woman in my life.'

'I'm seventy-six,' Mabel Dawkins told Lexi as she poured tea into bone china cups and nodded towards a plate of scones. 'Help yourselves. I always make scones when Kadir comes to tea. When he was a boy he could eat a plateful all to himself.'

Lexi settled back on the chintz sofa in Mabel's pretty apartment at the palace and bit into a feather-light fruit scone. 'So you were Kadir's nanny when he was growing up?'

'Lady Judith hired me when her son was born. After she left the palace and returned to England, Sultan Khalif asked me to remain here to give Kadir stability because it was a difficult situation for a young boy to grow up in two very different cultures, here in Zenhab and at Montgomery Manor in England.'

Lexi glanced at Kadir. 'It must have been strange to move between Western culture and Middle Eastern traditions. Do you think of yourself more as an English Earl or an Arab prince?'

'I love my mother and I was close to my grandfather, the tenth Earl. But I am my father's son, from an ancient line of desert kings, and my heart and soul belong to Zenhab,' he said without hesitation.

Recalling how, when they had arrived in Zenhab, Kadir had wielded a fearsome-looking sword and given a battle cry to rouse his horsemen, Lexi was learning that beneath his playboy image reported in the European press there was a far more serious side to the Sultan of Zenhab that the paparazzi never saw.

She was agonisingly conscious of him sitting next to her. The two-seater sofa was made even smaller because it was stuffed with Mabel's many crocheted cushions and, however stiffly Lexi held herself, she could not prevent her thigh from touching Kadir's. She could feel his hard muscles through her thin skirt, and the spicy tang of his cologne wove a seductive spell around her.

'What made you decide to join the RAF?' Mabel's voice dragged Lexi's mind away from her wayward thoughts.

She shrugged. 'I wanted an exciting career, the opportunity to travel.' She did not explain that one reason why she had joined the air force had been because she had been looking for somewhere where she felt she belonged. Her adoptive parents had not really wanted her, and she had been hurt that her birth mother had insisted on keeping her a secret from her husband, as if Cathy was ashamed of her.

'It must have been an exciting life, but dangerous too,' Mabel said. 'I expect your parents must have worried about you when you were stationed in Afghanistan.'

'I don't think so,' Lexi said wryly. 'My parents are busy with their own lives.'

'Kadir told me that you will be staying in Zenhab and working as his helicopter pilot for six months. That's a long time to be away from home, although I suppose when you were in the RAF you got used to living away from loved ones. Do you have a sweetheart back in England?'

Lexi was amused by the elderly nanny's curiosity. 'No, I don't.'

'I'm surprised. You're such a pretty girl. Are you gay?' Mabel asked bluntly.

Lexi choked on a mouthful of scone and hastily washed it down with a sip of tea. 'No, I'm not.' Realising that Mabel had no qualms about prying into her personal life, she murmured, 'Actually, I was engaged but it didn't work out.'

'Mabel, it's unfair to interrogate Lexi,' Kadir interrupted. He had felt the sudden tension that gripped her and forced himself to ignore his own curiosity about her love life. He recalled

Charles Fairfax had mentioned that she had been engaged but her fiancé had ended the relationship. Was she still in love with the guy she had hoped to marry? he mused, wondering why he disliked the idea.

His phone rang and he glanced at the name of the caller. 'I'll have to take this, I'm afraid,' he said apologetically. 'Lexi, please stay and finish your tea. If you think Mabel's scones are good, wait until you try her sponge cake.'

'He works so hard,' Mabel sighed when Kadir had left. 'He told me that his latest trip to Europe was very successful and he managed to secure several big deals with companies who will invest in new businesses in Zenhab.'

Lexi remembered that Kadir's adviser, Yusuf bin Hilal, had said that the Sultan worked hard to attract foreign investment to his kingdom. 'The European press seem more interested in Kadir's private life and his reputation as a playboy.'

'Oh, the press!' Mabel gave a snort. 'Most of what is written in the foreign newspapers is rubbish. The paparazzi don't know the man that I know Kadir to be. He vowed as his father lay dying that he would devote his life to Zenhab and continue Sultan Khalif's work to maintain peace and bring prosperity to the kingdom.'

'Was Kadir close to his father?'

'Very. Father and son adored one another.' Mabel's lined face softened. 'Kadir was heartbroken when Khalif died but at the same time he was relieved that his father was spared any more suffering.'

Lexi felt strangely unsettled at the thought of Kadir being heartbroken. She had been too ready to believe the stories in the tabloids about him leading a charmed life of hedonistic pleasure, she acknowledged guiltily. But she was discovering that he was a man of deep emotions who had grieved for his father and vowed to rule Zenhab with the same devotion to duty as Sultan Khalif had done. 'Why did Sultan Khalif suffer? Was he ill before he died?' she asked curiously.

'He suffered a stroke when Kadir was sixteen, which left him completely paralysed and barely able to speak. Obviously, Khalif could not continue to rule the country,' Mabel explained, 'and Kadir was too young to become Sultan, so Khalif's younger brother, Jamal, became the interim ruler until Kadir came of age.'

'And Jamal handed the Sultanate to Kadir when he was twenty-one?'

'Unfortunately, it wasn't quite as simple as that. Jamal wanted to remain as Sultan, and he had followers who believed that he should rule Zenhab and who were opposed to Kadir's plans to modernise the country. Before Jamal would agree to step aside and allow Kadir to take his rightful place as Sultan, he insisted that Kadir sign a contract to marry the daughter of Jamal's great ally, Sheikh Rashid bin Al-Hassan. Since Rashid died two months ago, Kadir has been under pressure to go ahead with his wedding to Princess Haleema to unite the country.

'Jamal and his followers are against change and want Zenhab to return to feudal isolation as it was in the past,' Mabel said grimly. 'There have been plots to overthrow Kadir, and two years ago he survived an assassination attempt. A gun was fired by someone in a crowd, but fortunately the bullet narrowly missed him.'

The conversation turned to other matters, but later, as Lexi walked in the palace gardens, she could not forget Mabel's revelation that an attempt had been made on Kadir's life by his enemies. Far from being the playboy prince she had believed him to be, he was a dutiful Sultan who had dedicated his life to his kingdom.

The sun was sliding below the horizon, staining the sky flamingo-pink, and the fiery hues were reflected in the ornamental pools and many fountains in the formal gardens.

Lexi strolled along an avenue of palm trees, but a familiar voice drew her from her thoughts, and her heart gave an annoying flip when she watched Kadir get up from a bench and walk towards her.

He had changed into a traditional white robe which skimmed his powerful body. As he came closer, Lexi could see the shadow of his black chest hairs beneath the fine cotton. He halted in front of her and smiled, revealing his perfect teeth, as white as his *keffiyeh* which framed his darkly tanned face.

'The gardens are so beautiful,' she said, looking around her because she dared not look at him, searching for something to say while she frantically tried to control her racing pulse.

'My father had them landscaped as a gift for my mother. She fell in love with the gardens at Versailles on their honeymoon and *Baba* wanted to re-create them at the palace. Unfortunately, the project took longer to complete than my parents' marriage lasted,' Kadir said drily.

He indicated a carving on the trunk of a palm tree, and Lexi saw the shape of a heart inscribed with the words *Judith will love Khalif for ever.* 'My mother made the carving. After she left, my father used to come and sit beneath this tree every day. He loved my mother until the day he died. When I look at the inscription I am reminded that people often do not mean what they say.'

'How true,' she said flatly, thinking of the many times people had let her down.

The emptiness in her voice stirred Kadir's curiosity. 'Why did your engagement end?'

For a moment Lexi did not answer. She rarely opened up about her private life. She did not understand the connection she felt with Kadir, but for some reason she felt drawn to confide in him.

'I met Steven when we were serving with the RAF in Afghanistan. Living in a war zone is a strange experience,' she explained ruefully. 'Your emotions are heightened by the constant threat of danger. When Steven proposed, I accepted because I longed for a settled life, a home and a family. We planned to marry as soon as we finished our tour of duty, but he had failed to mention that he had a girlfriend and a baby in England. He told me by text message on the evening that we were supposed to be holding our engagement party that he wasn't free to marry me.'

Beneath Lexi's tough exterior was a vulnerable woman who had been badly hurt, Kadir realised. He felt guilty that while they had been in Europe he had succumbed to the sexual chemistry between them and kissed her, knowing that he wasn't free to have any kind of relationship with her.

'Mabel reminded me that six months is a long time to be away from home,' he said abruptly. 'You are welcome to invite your friends and family to the palace. I thought you might like to ask your parents to visit.'

'They wouldn't want to come. But thanks for the offer.'

He was puzzled by her offhand response. 'It sounds as though you don't have a close relationship with your parents.'

Lexi shrugged. 'It's true that we're not close. I'm adopted. My parents believed they couldn't have a child but, after they adopted me, my mother fell pregnant and gave birth to a daughter, which rather made me redundant.'

Once again Kadir heard a note of hurt in her voice and he felt an unexpected tug on his heart. 'I'm sure your parents did not think that.'

'As a matter of fact I overheard Marcus tell another relative that he and Veronica—my adoptive mother—would not have adopted a child if they had known they could have a child of their own,' Lexi said flatly. 'From the age of eight I knew I was an inconvenience when my parents packed me off to boarding school so that they could concentrate on Athena.'

'I wondered why you and your sister do not look alike. Did you resent Athena because your parents gave her more attention?'

Lexi thought of her awkward, accident-prone sister and gave a rueful smile. 'It would be impossible to resent Athena. She has the sweetest nature, and actually I think she has struggled to meet Marcus and Veronica's expectations.' She frowned as she recalled her misgivings about Athena's intention to marry Charles Fairfax.

While she and Kadir had been talking, day had turned into night as quickly as Lexi remembered from the desert in Afghanistan, and a sliver of silver moon was climbing the sky accompanied by the first stars. She wondered what he was thinking. His hard-boned face was impossible to read, but she seemed to be acutely sensitive to his emotions and sensed that his mood had darkened.

'Tomorrow I will require you to fly me across the desert to the old city of Sanqirah in the mountains,' he said tersely. 'The northern territories are much hotter and drier than here, where we are closer to the coast. You will probably be more comfortable wearing appropriate clothing rather than your pilot's uniform.'

Lexi's stomach plummeted as if she was riding a big dipper at the funfair. She knew that Princess Haleema lived in the mountains. And Mabel had said that Kadir's uncle Jamal had been pushing for him to honour his marriage agreement. Pride demanded that she kept her voice unemotional. 'What time do you want to leave?'

'Early, and we won't return until late.' Kadir's jaw tightened. Since he had received a phone call from Haleema's brother, Omar, to confirm their meeting tomorrow he had sensed that his freedom was ending.

He felt no joy at the prospect of taking a girl he had never met as his bride, but it was necessary to prevent his detractors and Jamal's supporters from challenging his rule and creating civil unrest in the kingdom. The time had come for him to honour his promise to his father. But the future seemed bleaker since he had been plucked from the sea by a woman who challenged him at every opportunity and made his blood run faster through his veins.

'Lexi...' Kadir watched her walk away from him and could not prevent himself from uttering her name in a low, driven tone.

She turned to him, her face serenely beautiful. Her long blonde hair seemed to shimmer in the moonlight. 'Yes.'

Her voice was not quite steady, and Kadir

knew then that the night air, thick with the scents of jasmine and orange blossom, was bewitching her senses as it beguiled his. He saw wariness in her eyes as well as a hunger that she could not hide, and he knew he should walk away from her.

She had been hurt by her ex-fiancé and by her adoptive parents. He had no right to play with her emotions when he knew that it could only lead to him hurting her too. But she was so lovely. He had never wanted any woman as fiercely as he wanted her and he could not stop himself from walking towards her.

'Was there something else you wanted?' she asked innocently.

'Just…this…'

'*No.*' Lexi's soft cry was crushed by Kadir's mouth as he pulled her into his arms and claimed her lips. Her protest was carried away on the breeze that stirred the fronds of the palm trees. She had not expected him to kiss her and she had no time to muster any resistance, or so she tried to kid herself. But she was already lost to his magic, swept into his sensual spell as he swept her hard against him so that she was conscious of every muscle and sinew in his body, every beat of his heart.

His lips sipped from hers as he kissed her with a hunger that matched her own. Desire blazed white-hot, but underlying their passion was something indefinable, a connection between two souls as their two hearts thundered in unison.

Lexi gasped as Kadir skimmed his lips down her throat. The stubble on his jaw grazed her sensitive skin and the exquisite pleasure-pain sent a shudder through her. She arched her neck as he threaded his fingers into her hair and almost purred with pleasure when he cradled her head, angling her face so that he could plunder her mouth again and again until she felt boneless.

She could feel the solid ridge of his arousal pushing against her pelvis, and the evidence of his need excited her. But it was *wrong*. He had promised to marry another woman.

'No!' She tore her mouth from his, noting that he made no attempt to stop her. 'No more games,' she said quietly, proud that her voice was steady, even if her legs were not. Somehow she forced her feet to move, although it felt as if she had severed a limb when she stepped away from him. 'What do you want from me, Kadir?'

'Everything.'

The single word detonated between them as his harsh voice resonated with a depth of emotion that shocked Lexi. His eyes were black in the darkness. Kadir clenched his hands into fists to prevent himself from reaching for her. She could never be his and the knowledge felt like a knife blade through his heart. 'But I cannot take your beauty and your fire. And I can offer you nothing. I should not have brought you to Zenhab.'

The tortured expression on his face made Lexi's insides twist with a shared pain, and she suddenly knew that if she stayed in Zenhab they would destroy each other.

'Then let me go,' she whispered. 'This situation is unbearable for both of us. And it will be unfair on your young bride. Haleema may have led a sheltered life but she will notice the way we look at each other.' She swallowed. 'Steven made me an unwitting accomplice when he cheated on his girlfriend who was waiting for him in England. Our desire for one another is wrong, and the only way we can end it is for me to leave Zenhab and we will never see each other again.' The thought was agonising, but Lexi knew it would be even more painful to remain at the palace and watch Kadir marry his Princess.

Lexi was right. He had to let her go, Kadir acknowledged heavily. His duty to his kingdom and his promise to his father must come before his personal desires. 'I still need you to fly me to Haleema's home in the mountains tomorrow. My meeting with her brother, Sheikh Omar, is arranged and it will be seen as a great insult if I fail to attend. But after that I will release you from your contract…and you will be free to leave Zenhab,' he said harshly.

It was for the best, Lexi told herself. The madness had to end. Without a word, she turned and fled from Kadir, her chest aching with the leaden weight of her heart. As she ran through the dark gardens she did not notice one of the palace staff watching her from the shadows.

CHAPTER EIGHT

THE SULTAN WAS dressed in his robes of state, although he was not carrying a sword or a ceremonial knife in his belt, Lexi noted. The embroidered jacket he wore over his white robe was encrusted with dark red rubies which reminded her of droplets of blood.

She gave herself a mental shake, impatient with her fanciful imagination. But she could not tear her gaze from Kadir as he walked across the palace courtyard to the helipad, and she was conscious of his gaze skimming over her desert boots, khaki combats and vest top. She had tied her hair into a ponytail and the peak of her baseball cap cast a shadow over her face which she hoped disguised the dark circles beneath her eyes, evidence of her sleepless night.

'You said I didn't need to wear my pilot's uniform,' she reminded him, taking his silence as censure.

'You should bring a jacket. The temperature in the mountains can drop twenty degrees once the sun sets in the evening.'

Silence stretched between them, tightening Lexi's nerves. She could still taste him on her lips from when he had kissed her the previous night. 'Is it safe for you to go to the mountains?' she burst out. 'Mabel said that the northern tribes are your enemies and there has already been one attempt made on your life.'

His brows rose 'Why, Lexi, would you care if someone took a pot shot at me?' he drawled.

In her mind, she was back in Helmand province in Afghanistan, watching her co-pilot Sam jump out of the helicopter and run to the aid of an injured soldier. The sniper's bullet seemed to come from nowhere. One second Sam was running, the next he was lying lifeless on the desert sand. Death had been delivered in the blink of an eye. Lexi would always remember Sam's cheerful grin and zest for life.

She stared at the blood-red rubies spattered over Kadir's jacket and pictured a faceless figure in a crowd, aiming a gun and pulling the trigger. 'Of course I'd care, damn you,' she said thickly.

'Lexi.' Kadir swore beneath his breath.

She turned away from him, afraid he would see the raw emotions he evoked in her. 'Why do you have a different bodyguard?' She glanced at the man sitting in the front passenger seat of the helicopter. 'Where are Nasim and Ashar?'

'Ashar is away visiting his family. Nasim called in sick this morning.'

Lexi frowned. 'What's wrong with him? He seemed fine in the gym yesterday.'

Kadir closed his eyes and tried to dismiss the vision of Lexi's bottom in tight pink shorts moving up and down as she performed push-ups in a competition with his bodyguard. 'Your concern for Nasim is touching,' he said curtly. 'But no doubt you will strike up a friendship with Fariq.'

'I'm not so sure.' Lexi couldn't explain why she had not warmed to the replacement bodyguard, or why her nerves felt on edge. She looked around the empty courtyard. 'Where are Yusuf and your other advisers who usually accompany you?'

'I am going to the mountains alone, and I am not carrying my ceremonial weapons to show my host, Sheikh Omar, that I come in peace.' By the end of today he would be officially engaged to Haleema and Zenhab would be looking forward to a royal wedding, Kadir thought with grim resignation.

Lexi held open the door of the helicopter

and was gripped by an inexplicable sense of dread. 'I've got a bad feeling about this trip.' She shrugged helplessly. 'I wish we weren't going today.'

For a split second, emotion flickered in Kadir's dark gaze, a look almost of pain, before his thick lashes swept down like curtains hiding the windows to his soul.

'I have to go,' he said harshly. 'This is my destiny.' He glanced at the gold watch on his wrist. 'It's time we were on our way.'

The AgustaWestland was a dream to fly, and once Lexi had taken off she turned the helicopter towards the desert and prepared to enjoy the spectacular view. Beside her, the new bodyguard seemed restless and ill at ease and although the cabin was air-conditioned he was sweating profusely.

Lexi glanced at him. 'Are you nervous about flying, Fariq?' she asked him, speaking into her headset.

'No. *I'm* not afraid, but you should be.'

Puzzled, she turned her head to look at him and her heart catapulted against her ribs when she saw a gleam of grey metal and recognised the barrel of a pistol partly concealed in the bodyguard's jacket. 'Don't make a fuss,' Fariq said softly. 'Fly the helicopter to these new co-ordinates.'

Lexi glanced at the piece of paper he placed on her knee. On the video screen she could see Kadir in the rear of the helicopter, putting on his headphones, and she guessed he was unaware of the situation. Her eyes jerked to the pistol that Fariq was aiming at her ribs. Her mouth felt dry, but her military training kicked in and she suppressed her fear by forcing herself to think logically and remain calm.

Moments later, Kadir's voice came though her headphones. 'Why are you heading towards the coast? You're flying in the wrong direction.'

The bodyguard turned around and pointed the gun at Kadir. 'There has been a change of plan, Your Highness. Hand over your cellphones, both of you.'

Kadir froze, and his first thought was that he should have questioned, as Lexi had, the fact that Nasim had unexpectedly been taken ill. Clearly, someone had wanted his protection officer out of the way and he prayed that Nasim had not been killed.

'Whatever it is you want, there is no reason for you to involve my pilot.' He spoke calmly to Fariq. 'Let Lexi land the helicopter. You can keep me as a hostage, or kill me if that is your plan. But let her go.'

'*No!*' Lexi felt a rush of emotion at Kadir's attempt to protect her. 'You can't kill the Sultan,' she told the gunman. 'You'll never get away with it. If you allow him to go free, I'll fly you to wherever you want to go and no one will know about this incident.'

Fariq laughed. 'Your determination to protect each other is touching,' he sneered. He stared at Kadir. 'The rumour that the western woman is your mistress is obviously correct. Nobody will get killed as long as you do as I tell you. Continue flying to the coordinates I gave you,' the gunman ordered Lexi, 'and don't try anything clever because I swear I will pull the trigger and we'll all go down.'

She could tell he meant what he said, and she could also tell he was nervous, which made him volatile and likely to panic. There was nothing Lexi could do but fly to the new destination. After fifteen minutes, during which time the mounting tension seemed to suck the air out of the cabin, they flew over the coast.

The sea was sapphire-blue and sparkled in the early morning sunshine. Did the world seem more beautiful because she had a gun aimed at her? Lexi wondered. She was conscious of her heart beating hard and fast in her chest as adrenalin pumped through her veins.

On the video screen she could see Kadir sitting behind her. What if the gunman did actually intend to kill him?

Fear stole her breath. *She could not bear to lose him!* She couldn't bear to kneel by his lifeless body as she had knelt beside her best friend, Sam, desperately searching for a pulse but knowing it was too late.

Kadir is not yours to lose, whispered a voice in her head. And in a heartbeat she discovered that she wished he was.

Below them, a small island came into view, white sand and green palm trees rising up out of the sapphire sea. 'Land the chopper down there on the beach,' the gunman instructed.

Would they be ambushed by more gunmen once they were on the ground? Supremely conscious of the pistol barrel inches away from her, Lexi took the helicopter down and landed it on the beach.

'Now get out, both of you, and put your hands above your heads.'

Lexi jumped down onto the sand and raised her arms, and seconds later she was joined by Kadir. The gunman seemed to be working alone. She scanned the line of trees at the top of the beach and saw no sign of anyone else.

'I reckon we could take him,' she muttered to Kadir. 'We're two against one.'

'But the one has a gun,' he hissed back. 'Don't be stupid.'

His words had the desired effect, Kadir noted with relief as Lexi's eyes flashed him a furious look. She was as courageous as a tigress, but no way would he allow her to risk her life. He was confused by their location. Nothing made sense, and the situation became even more bizarre when the gunman locked the helicopter and pocketed the key.

Fariq ran down the beach, and it was then that Lexi noticed a motorboat half hidden behind some rocks. She watched Fariq push the boat into the sea before he leapt aboard and started the engine.

'He's leaving us here!' Her brain finally clicked into gear. Events had happened so quickly, but now Lexi stared at the boat as it sped away. *'Hey...'*

She spun round to Kadir. 'Terrific, we're stranded. From the air, the island looked uninhabited. But why would the gunman leave us here? Surely when you fail to arrive for your meeting with Haleema's brother, an alert will be raised that you are missing and people will search for you? What can anyone hope to gain by kidnapping us and dumping us on a deserted island?'

Kadir racked his brain for an explanation.

Someone did not want him to meet Omar bin Al-Hassan to discuss his marriage to Princess Haleema, but who, and why? The only reason he could think of was that the person behind the kidnap plot did not want him to make peace with the leader of the northern tribes. Someone wanted to stir up trouble in Zenhab, and the most obvious suspect was his uncle. He dragged his mind from his confused thoughts as Lexi started to stride along the beach. 'Where are you going?'

She glanced over her shoulder. 'To find somewhere for us to shelter; it's the first thing I learned to do in RAF survival training. From the air I saw some cliffs on the other side of the island, and there might be a cave. We'll also need to find food, and collect firewood.'

Kadir hid his irritation that his pilot was too bossy for her own good and sat down on a rock. 'It sounds exhausting,' he drawled.

Lexi put her hands on her hips, her slender body practically quivering with impatience. 'Are you just going to sit there? You might be a Sultan, but if you think I'm going to wait on you like your staff at the palace do, think again.'

She marched away from him, her temper fizzing. But she recognised that her anger was a release of her pent-up emotions. She felt sick with relief that the gunman had not hurt them. Fear had churned in her stomach when the gun had been pointed at her, and she'd been terrified when the gunman had aimed at Kadir. Now, for some reason, she felt stupidly tearful and she was fighting a strong urge to run back to Kadir and throw herself into his arms.

The island was bigger than it had looked from the air and it took Lexi almost two hours to follow the coastline round to the other side, where she found a few low cliffs and no caves. She continued walking for another hour before completing a circuit of the island and finally ended up back at the helicopter. There was no sign of Kadir and, after dumping the driftwood she had collected to make a fire, she walked up the beach and into the shade of the palm trees. The ground was littered with branches and palm fronds that could be used to construct a shelter, she decided.

Pushing through the trees, she found herself at the edge of a desert plain. Beyond a line of dunes she could see more palm trees and the glint of water—an oasis, and next to it…a tent!

What on earth? Ignoring the fact that she was hot and tired from hours of walking in the burning sun, Lexi scrambled over the dunes, her progress hampered by her feet sinking into the soft sand. She was breathless when she arrived at the huge tent and stared in disbelief at Kadir lying on a hammock strung between two palm trees.

'Where *are* we?' She was beginning to feel as if she had fallen into the pages of *Alice in Wonderland.*

Kadir propped himself up on one elbow and regarded her lazily. He had changed out of his royal robes into a pair of frayed denim shorts that sat low on his hips and displayed his muscle-packed abdomen. Beneath the glare of the desert sun, his bare chest was the colour of burnished bronze overlaid with whorls of silky black hairs.

Lexi licked her parched lips, conscious that her pounding heart was not the result of walking over the dunes.

'We're on Jinan, which means beautiful garden,' he told her. 'It is a private island belonging to me personally, rather than to the Sultanate of Zenhab.'

'Why did the kidnapper bring us to your private island?' Lexi frowned as the meaning of his words became clear. 'You must have known where we were when I landed the helicopter. Why did you let me traipse around the island looking for a place to shelter when you knew that this—' she waved towards the tent '—was here?'

He shrugged and his powerful shoulder muscles rippled beneath his satiny skin. 'You were determined to demonstrate your survival techniques and it seemed a shame to spoil your fun.'

In truth, Kadir had felt relieved when she'd stormed off along the beach. He had needed some time alone to control his emotions in the aftermath of seeing a gun being aimed at Lexi. When her life had been threatened on the helicopter he had been consumed with rage, but his desperation to protect her had been tempered by the bitter realisation that the kidnapper was quite literally calling the shots.

Lexi glared at him, her temper flaring as quickly as tinder set alight with a match. 'Bastard!' Her blue eyes blazed as she walked towards him and Kadir tensed as he watched her pull a penknife from the pocket of her combats. Without uttering another word, she sliced through the rope which tied one end of the hammock to the tree trunk and watched him land in an ignominious heap on the sand before she strode into the tent.

It was the size of a marquee, Lexi realised as she looked around the interior of the tent. Camping on Dartmoor on military exercises with the RAF had *never* been like this! She pulled off her boots and walked barefoot across the richly patterned rugs covering the floor. In place of chairs and sofas there was a raised platform covered with brightly coloured fabric and sumptuous silk cushions. Drawing aside a curtain, she discovered a bedroom with a huge, low bed draped with satin sheets in vibrant jewel shades. Behind a partition was a bathroom with a walk-in shower and at the far end of the tent was a kitchen area complete with a working fridge.

'Solar panels provide electricity, and the oasis is a source of fresh water,' Kadir explained as he followed her into the kitchen and opened the fridge to take out a bottle of drink. 'I keep a satellite phone here, but the kidnappers have taken it so we can't call for help,' he said in answer to Lexi's questioning look.

He watched her gnaw her bottom lip with her teeth and the giveaway sign of her vulnerability touched him more than it had any right to. 'I don't believe that whoever is behind the kidnap plot intends to harm us, because they would have done so by now. For some reason, someone wants me out of the way for a while.' He frowned. 'I have an idea who is behind this.' Jamal's weasel features came into his mind. 'But at the moment I don't understand why.'

'What if we are left stranded here for weeks?'

'That won't happen. My staff come to the island regularly to check on the place, and there is always a supply of non-perishable food here, certainly enough to last us for a few days before we have to go hunting for our meals.'

The amusement in his voice was the last straw. 'I can't believe I was actually worried that the kidnapper might hurt you,' Lexi snapped. 'I walked around the island for three goddamned *hours* while you were lazing here in luxury.' As she spoke, she swept her arms around the tent. 'I could *kill* you!'

Her hand collided with the glass Kadir held out to her, showering him in pomegranate juice. 'Oh, I'm sorry.' She stared at the rivers of red liquid running down his face and chest. The dark red juice looked like blood.

If the kidnapper had fired the gun at Kadir... The thought made her feel ill. 'I...I didn't mean that.' Her voice shook. She tried to firm her trembling mouth, but her lips wouldn't stop wobbling. 'I was scared on the helicopter,' she admitted.

'You, scared?' Kadir's voice sounded strained. 'Never. You are the bravest, craziest woman I've ever met.'

Suddenly Lexi did not care if she was revealing too much of herself. 'I was scared the kidnapper would kill you.'

'I would have ripped the gunman apart with my bare hands if he had tried to harm you,' Kadir said roughly. The shimmer of tears in her eyes tore him apart. His self-control exploded and he muttered a savage imprecation as he hauled her into his arms, crushing the air from her lungs as he lifted her and held her so tightly to him that Lexi felt the urgent thud of his heart beating in time with her own.

The threat of death had brought home to Lexi the immeasurable value of life. She had been running from the truth and trying to hide her feelings for Kadir, but she could not run or hide any longer.

She felt detached from reality, cast adrift in a world where only the two of them existed. The feel of his warm skin beneath her hands heated her blood, and the feral hunger glittering in his eyes evoked an ache in the pit of her stomach. She curled her arms around his neck and buried her fingers in his silky dark hair as he lowered his head and captured her mouth, kissing her urgently as if he was slaking his thirst after being stranded in the desert without water for many days.

His lips tasted of pomegranate juice, and the sticky juice running down his chest transferred to her. But Lexi did not care; all she cared about was that he should not stop the sensual sorcery he was creating with his tongue inside her mouth. She was only vaguely aware of him striding across the tent into the bathroom, and she gasped as he turned on the shower and stepped beneath the spray with her in his arms.

'I've still got my clothes on,' she muttered against his lips.

'Not for much longer,' he promised.

He let her slide down him so that she was standing on her feet, and whipped her vest top over her head. 'No bra,' he growled in satisfaction, cupping her firm breasts that he had bared.

'It's too hot to wear one.' She caught her breath as he rolled her nipples between his fingers until they hardened to turgid points and starbursts of sensation arrowed from her breasts to the pit of her stomach. His tanned hands splayed over her creamy pale breasts, caressing their rounded shape before he lowered his head and closed his lips around one nipple, suckling her strongly until she gave a moan of pleasure. He judged the exact moment when she could withstand no more of the exquisite caress, and moved to her other nipple, lashing the taut peak with his tongue, back and forth, tormenting her so that she gripped his hair and held his head to her breast in a silent plea for him to ravish her eager flesh.

'You are so damned beautiful, you're driving me crazy,' Kadir said harshly. 'When I thought the kidnapper might kill me, all I could think was that I was going to die without ever knowing the sensual promise of your body.'

In those seconds when he had faced his mortality the only person in his mind had been Lexi, and she consumed his thoughts now, making Kadir forget his responsibilities as Sultan, his duty to his kingdom and the promise he had made to his father. Time had halted, the universe had stopped spinning, and nothing mattered but the woman who had haunted his thoughts and dreams since he had met her.

His hands shook as he fumbled with the zip of Lexi's combats and pushed them over her hips. While she was stepping out of her trousers he hooked his fingers in the waistband of her briefs and dragged them down her thighs, his impatient fingers skimming over the neat triangle of blonde hair to part her and probe her silken heat.

'You want me.' His dark eyes gleamed with triumph, but Lexi could not deny her need when the wetness of her arousal betrayed her. Kadir gave a soft laugh as he slid one finger deep inside her, stretched her a little and inserted a second finger, swirling them in an erotic dance that drew a husky moan from her.

He handed her a bar of soap and Lexi smoothed it over his chest to wash away the sticky pomegranate juice. Now it was her turn to feel triumphant as she dragged her knuckles down his stomach and felt his body shudder. With deft fingers she opened the fly of his shorts and tugged the wet denim down his thighs before repeating the action with his black silk boxers. The size of his erection caused her a moment's panic. He was beautiful, and *huge*, and her insides turned to liquid as she imagined taking him inside her.

Kadir gritted his teeth as Lexi stroked her fingers lightly up and down his shaft, teasing him with butterfly caresses that increased the blood flow to his swollen tip. In retribution he circled his thumb pad over the tight bud of her clitoris and simultaneously circled his tongue around a dusky pink nipple.

The effect was electric; she trembled and gave a keening cry which he caught in his mouth as he lifted her up and claimed her lips in a slow, sweet kiss that made his gut ache. Her unguarded response stirred his soul. Something about this strong woman coming apart so utterly in his arms humbled him and at the same time he felt like a king who had captured a thousand kingdoms.

She wrapped her legs around his waist as he carried her out of the shower. The drumbeat of desire pounded harder in his veins. 'I can't wait,' he groaned, feeling the storm inside him building to a crescendo.

Lexi smiled against his mouth. Nothing mattered but that they were alive and she wanted to celebrate life in the most fundamental way, by making love with the man who had captured her heart. 'I can't wait either,' she whispered. She could feel his arousal nudging her belly and she wanted him inside her now, *now*...

Kadir stood her on her feet and turned her around so that her back was against his chest. There was a chair in the bathroom. He placed it in front of her and gently pushed her forward so that her body formed an arch over the wooden backrest and her hands rested on the seat. She was still wearing her baseball cap, and he pulled it from her head so that her long blonde hair cascaded around her shoulders like a river of silk.

'Hold on,' he murmured and felt a quiver run through her as he smoothed his hands over her perfect peachy bottom. The memory of her doing push-ups in a pair of tight satin shorts shattered the last vestige of his restraint and with a harsh groan he eased her buttocks apart and thrust deep into her moist heat, where his fingers had aroused her moments earlier.

Sweet heaven… Lexi could not hold back a cry of pleasure as Kadir entered her. Nothing had prepared her for the incredible eroticism of stretching forwards over the chair while he stood behind her and drove his powerful erection into the heat of her femininity. Nor had she been prepared for the intensity of emotions she felt as their bodies joined and became one.

He leaned forward and kissed the tip of her ear. She turned her head and sought his mouth and he kissed her with passion and a heart-shaking tenderness that answered a deeper need inside her.

He began to move, slowly at first to allow her to accommodate his size. Lexi gripped the edge of the chair as he increased his rhythm, each measured stroke building her excitement and her anticipation that the best was yet to come.

She spread her legs wider, encouraging him to drive deeper and harder. He wrapped his arms around her waist, cocooning her with his big body, and drew gasps of delight from her when he played with her nipples, heightening her sensual pleasure until she trembled and shivered with each new sensation created by his skilful mastery.

It couldn't last. The fire of their mutual passion swiftly became a furnace that blazed out of control. Lexi was vaguely aware of panting breaths and realised it was the sound of her breath being torn from her lungs as she strove to reach the pinnacle. Kadir held her there for breathless seconds, making her wait for the rapture of release. And then he thrust into her the hardest yet and sent them both tumbling over the edge into ecstasy. She cried his name and he soothed her with soft words in Arabic, his voice deep as an ocean as emotions he had not expected to feel, knew he should not feel, rolled over him.

As Kadir withdrew from her, Lexi's legs gave way and he swept her up in his arms and carried her into the bedroom. The satin sheets felt cool against her burning skin as he laid her on the bed. She stared up at him and held her hand to his cheek, traced the shape of his beautiful mouth with her fingertips. His smile stole her breath and the sultry gleam in his eyes warned her that he had by no means finished.

'Already?' She could not hide her shock as he knelt above her and pushed her legs apart. 'You're insatiable.'

'Insatiable for you,' he whispered against her lips before he kissed her deeply and made love to her again with such exquisite care that Lexi felt a sense of belonging she had been searching for her whole life.

CHAPTER NINE

SOMETHING WAS BRUSHING softly across her face. Lexi opened her eyes and discovered the mosquito net draped around the bed was fluttering in the breeze wafting into the tent. She was alone in the semi-dark. The luminous dial on her watch revealed that it was early evening, which meant that she had slept all afternoon. It was not surprising after her energetic sex session with Kadir, she thought. Her face warmed as she recalled how he had made love to her bent over the chair in the bathroom, and twice again in a variety of erotic positions on the bed.

Where was he? Fear gripped her as she wondered if the kidnapper had returned and taken Kadir away at gunpoint. *Perhaps the gunman had killed him?* Heart hammering, she slid off the satin sheets. There was a shirt draped over the arm of the chair; she assumed it belonged to Kadir and slipped it on before she stepped cautiously out of the bedroom, wishing she had a weapon to defend herself with if the kidnapper had indeed returned.

She walked noiselessly into the living area and found it empty. The tent flap had been tied back and through the opening she saw Kadir standing next to the oasis, staring up at the sky that was rapidly darkening as the sun completely disappeared. The heavens were filling with silver stars, like pins on a velvet pincushion. The wondrous beauty of the cosmos was displayed in breathtaking magnificence and, standing in the vast desert beneath the vast sky, Lexi thought how insignificant the human race was.

'My father loved to watch the stars.' Kadir turned as Lexi approached, sensing her presence although she made no sound. 'Many nights when I was a boy we sat outside the tent and *Baba* taught me the constellations.'

'You came to Jinan with him?'

'Yes, it was a special place for both of us, away from the palace and the many duties of a Sultan. Here we were simply father and son, and we used to go fishing and cook what we caught. My father taught me to enjoy the simple things in life.'

'Everyone I've spoken to says that Sultan

Khalif was a great ruler of Zenhab,' Lexi said softly.

'He was the salvation of the kingdom.' Kadir's voice was fierce with pride. 'Before my father became Sultan, Zenhab was riven by civil war. He worked hard to establish peace and he gave hope for the future, but only if the population were willing to embrace change and welcome ideologies from the outside world.' His jaw clenched. 'There are still some people in Zenhab who want to return to the old ways.' Always he came back to the thorn in his side—Jamal—he brooded.

'You loved your father.' Lexi's voice pulled Kadir from his dark thoughts about his uncle. 'It's sad that he died when you were a young man and you did not have more time with him.' She felt a tug on her heart, remembering how Kadir's old nanny, Mabel, had said his heart had been broken by Sultan Khalif's death. 'At least you had a loving father while you were growing up. Mabel said the Sultan adored you.'

Kadir heard the wistful note in her voice and pictured her as a little girl whose adoptive parents had sent her away to boarding school so that they could concentrate on their own daughter.

'How old were you when you were adopted?'

'Four.'

He frowned. 'So, did you spend the first years of your life with your real parents?'

'No, I was placed into social services' care soon after I was born. Apparently I was fostered by a couple who planned to adopt me, but some time during the adoption process they changed their mind and I went back into care until the Howards adopted me two years later. I was too young to remember any of those experiences, of course.'

As an adult, Lexi had read various articles about attachment issues which could affect adopted children and the psychological problems resulting from negative early life experiences which could last into adulthood. The first failed adoption, followed by her failure to bond with the Howards was likely to be the reason why she was fiercely independent, yet deep down she wished she'd had a close, loving relationship like Kadir had enjoyed with his father. She'd been accused of pushing people away. It was true that she was wary of allowing anyone too close, she acknowledged. And when she *had* lowered her barriers with Steven, he had betrayed her trust.

Caught up in her thoughts, Lexi had only been partly aware that Kadir had led her back inside the tent. 'I thought you must be hungry,' he said, indicating the trays of food set out on the raised platform. He dropped down onto the piles of cushions and indicated that she should do the same. 'It's only crackers and dried fruits, I'm afraid.'

Lexi scanned the picnic and realised she was starving. 'It looks wonderful,' she assured him, biting into a plump dried fig. 'It reminds me of the midnight feasts we used to have at boarding school, only we had to eat in the dark because if we were caught by the housemistress it meant a week of detentions.'

Kadir thought of his own generally happy years at Eton College. The only downside had been that he had hated being separated from his father. 'What did you think of boarding school?'

'It was hard at first, but I got used to sleeping in a dormitory and only going home for the school holidays. In many ways it toughened me up.'

'Did you need to toughen up? You were eight years old,' he said softly. With her pale blonde hair falling around her beautiful face she looked fragile and ethereal, but he knew she had a backbone of steel.

She shrugged. 'It helped. After a while I stopped caring that my adoptive parents didn't love me.'

'What about your biological parents? Have you ever tried to trace them?'

'No,' she said abruptly. She did not want to tell him that her birth mother had been a prostitute when she had conceived Lexi.

She wondered how the Sultan of Zenhab would react if she told him he had spent the afternoon having sex with the daughter of a whore. Keen to turn the subject away from her private life, Lexi focused on the meal he had prepared.

'This is *baklava*, isn't it?' she said, picking up a little pastry. 'Layers of dough stuffed with pistachio nuts and honey. I tried them once before when I was serving in the Middle East and I remember they were delicious.'

'They're even better if you dip them in honey,' Kadir told her, pushing a bowl of thick golden liquid towards her.

She dipped the pastry into the honey and popped it into her mouth. A rapturous expression crossed her face. 'Mmm, I admit I have a weakness for sweet things.'

Kadir watched the tip of her pink tongue dart out to capture a crumb of pastry. She reminded him of a contented kitten, and her sensual enjoyment of the cake aroused a barbaric need in him to push her back against the cushions and thrust his throbbing erection deep inside her welcoming heat. He knew she would be ready for him. Her blue eyes—no longer chips of ice, but smoky-soft—had been issuing an invitation since she had stood beside him at the oasis.

'You've got honey on your chin,' he murmured as he lowered his head towards her. 'And as there are no napkins I'll have to lick it off you.'

Her impish smile tugged on something deep inside him. For a few seconds he glimpsed the child who had grown too serious too soon.

'I would be grateful if you would,' she murmured, as demure as a Victorian maiden. But Kadir had a vivid memory of earlier, when she had pushed him down on the bed and positioned herself above him, deliberately tormenting him as she had slowly, oh-so slowly, lowered herself onto his erect shaft before riding him hard and fast.

His breath hissed between his teeth as he struggled to control his hunger. His hand was already untying the belt of his silk robe, revealing his swollen manhood, and her little gasp when she saw how aroused he was drove him beyond rational thought.

It was impossible to rationalise anything that had happened since they had flown away from the palace that morning, Kadir brooded. Those moments on the helicopter when he had looked at death down the barrel of a gun had evoked a feeling of urgency to reaffirm life. He was aware that this was one stolen night. For a few hours, the past and the future did not exist and there was only now, with this woman. He could not fight his need for Lexi.

He brushed his lips over hers and his heart kicked when he felt her instant response. 'You taste sweet,' he growled, sliding his tongue into her mouth to explore her with mind-blowing eroticism that left them both shaking.

Lexi tasted salt on his skin when she kissed his throat. In the glow from the oil lamp his broad shoulders gleamed like polished gold, and his dark chest hairs felt abrasive against her palms as she ran her hands down his body, over his flat stomach and lower to clasp the rigid length of his erection.

His hands were no less busy opening the buttons down the front of her shirt and sliding the material from her shoulders so that she was naked beneath his glittering gaze. She made a startled protest when he dipped his fingers into the bowl of honey and trickled the sticky syrup over her breasts. He laughed at her surprise before closing his lips around one honey-coated nipple and suckling her until she sobbed his name.

'Sticky and sweet,' he murmured, transferring his mouth to her other honey-anointed breast and curling his tongue around its taut peak. 'From now on I will always be addicted to the taste of honey.'

It was sensuality taken to another level and before long Lexi was squirming and arching her hips in mute supplication for him to assuage the ache between her legs.

'Patience, *habibi*,' he teased. 'Let me discover if you taste sweet here, too.'

She shivered with anticipation as he hooked her legs over his shoulders and slid his hands beneath her bottom, lifting her as he lowered his head and pressed his mouth against her to taste her molten heat with his tongue.

The intimate caress felt unbelievably good. Lexi was lost from the first lick of Kadir's tongue up and down her moist opening, as he delicately but determinedly probed and delved and finally thrust into her feminine heat. Her body arched like a bow under intolerable tension, quivering as the pleasure inside her built. She curled her fingers into the satin cushions beneath her as he curled his tongue around her clitoris and created a storm of sensations that were too exquisite for her to withstand.

She exploded in a frantic orgasm, her hips jerking towards his wicked mouth, her breath forced from her lungs so that her gasps of pleasure filled the tent. It was impossible that anything could be better than what he had just done to her, but then he lifted his head and stood between her spread thighs to drive his powerful erection deep inside her, and Lexi began the delicious journey to nirvana all over again.

Lexi turned her head on the pillow and studied Kadir while he slept. The chiselled angles of his face looked softer, and his thick black lashes made crescents on his cheeks. Last night he had called her *habibi*, which she knew was an Arabic term of endearment, and when he had made love to her she had sensed tenderness as well as passion in his caresses. Had they simply had sex, she mused, or was it possible that he cared for her a little?

Dear heaven! What had they done?

She jolted fully awake, and the dreamy smile on her lips disappeared. Last night had been no dream. Of course he could not care for her. She and Kadir had had sex, but their passion was forbidden and they should not have become lovers. She glanced around the tent, filled with warm golden sunlight, and a chill spread through her body as cold reality hit her.

She had been flying Kadir to meet his fiancée when they had been kidnapped and stranded on the island. It was true that Kadir's arranged marriage was no love match. He had never even met Haleema. But he was contracted to marry the Princess, and they should not have allowed themselves to be swept away by passion, Lexi thought bleakly.

Her heart was beating so hard that she was sure she could hear it. She frowned when she realised that the sound came from a long way off and she recognised the low throb of a motorboat's engine. *Perhaps the kidnapper had returned to the island.* Their lives could once again be in danger.

'Kadir.'

His lashes lifted, and his smooth chocolate eyes regarded her slumberously. 'I thought I was dreaming.' He cupped her breasts in his hands and gave her a sinful smile. 'But these feel real.'

Fear made Lexi momentarily forget her feelings of guilt. 'I can hear a boat engine,' she said urgently.

He dropped his hands from her body and leapt out of bed, frowning as he heard a faint thrumming sound. 'Stay here,' he ordered, dragging on his shorts. 'Find somewhere safe to hide while I go and see what's happening.'

'You must be joking!' It took seconds to pull

on her combats, but longer to wriggle her feet
into her boots and tie the laces. 'Wait for me!'
She cursed as he strode out of the tent, but
common sense warned her not to run across
the desert in bare feet and risk being bitten
by a highly venomous death stalker scorpion.

Adrenalin pumped through Kadir as he hid
behind a palm tree and watched a motorboat
land on the beach. No doubt the kidnapper was
still armed with a gun. He glanced around for
something he could use to defend himself with.
A tree branch would not be much use against
a pistol, he thought ruefully, but he had the
element of surprise combined with an implacable
determination to protect Lexi from the
gunman.

Shielding his eyes against the bright sun,
Kadir frowned as he recognised the man.
'Nasim!'

'Sir!' The bodyguard tore up the beach and
dropped down onto one knee before his Sultan.
'Your Highness, I feared Jamal might have
had you killed.'

'I guessed my uncle was behind this,' Kadir
said grimly. 'Do you know what he is up to?'

'He intends to depose you and make himself
Sultan, and he has a few followers, including
Fariq, working for him. I was held at

gunpoint but I managed to escape. I overheard that Jamal planned for you and Miss Howard to be kidnapped and brought to the island. Your uncle has gone to the mountains to inform Sheikh Omar that, instead of attending the meeting to discuss your marriage to Princess Haleema, you chose to come to Jinan with your mistress.

'Jamal has spies at the palace, and one of them reported that he had seen you kissing Lexi,' Nasim explained when Kadir frowned. 'Jamal hopes that Sheikh Omar will believe that you have snubbed his sister, and he will incite the mountain tribes to join forces with your uncle to overthrow you.'

Kadir's jaw clenched. 'I must act quickly. It is time I dealt with my uncle once and for all.' He looked round to see Lexi running across the sand. After giving instructions to his bodyguard, he walked up the beach towards her.

'What is Nasim doing here? He's not working for the kidnapper, is he?' she demanded.

'He came to rescue us. As I suspected, my uncle is behind the kidnap plot.' Kadir threw her the helicopter keys. 'I need you to take me to the mountains to visit Haleema, and there is no time to lose. Wait here while I go and shut up the tent.'

Lexi stared after him as he strode up the

beach and bit her lip. She did not know what she had expected from him, but his absolute indifference to the fact that they had spent the night together made her feel used and humiliated. His urgency to visit Haleema emphasised how unimportant she was to him, Lexi thought bitterly, just as she had been unimportant to her adoptive parents.

What the hell had he done?

As Kadir ploughed over the soft sand dunes, the sated ache in his groin was a mocking reminder of exactly what he had done to Lexi last night, and what she had done to him. She had made him forget *everything* except the thunder in his blood, his urgent, uncontrollable need to make love to her. But he could not blame Lexi for the fact that he had broken his promise to himself. And, despite the fact that he had just enjoyed the most amazing night of his life with her, he could not break the promise he had made to his father.

He heard Sultan Khalif's voice inside his head.

'The marriage arrangement that Jamal has brokered between you and the daughter of the leader of the northern tribes will ensure stability in the kingdom. The people of Zenhab deserve peace and prosperity after years of war

and bloodshed. It is my dying wish, my only son, that when the time comes you will honour your promise to take Princess Haleema as your bride.'

Stumbling into the tent, Kadir sank to his knees and dropped his head into his hands as if he could somehow hold back the tidal wave of emotions rolling over him. Shame tasted as bitter as poison in his mouth. By making love to Lexi he had betrayed his personal code of honour and he had betrayed his father. It was no comfort that he had not technically had sex with Lexi in Zenhab and they had been on his private island, Jinan.

Even worse than letting himself down was the realisation that Lexi hoped, perhaps even expected, that having sex with her had meant something to him. Her soft smile when she had run towards him on the beach just now had made his gut twist, and the look of disappointment on her face when she'd realised that they could leave the island had been more revealing than perhaps she knew.

He cursed savagely, anger and guilt mingling with his shame. *He did not want to hurt Lexi.* The discovery shocked him. His many previous affairs had been with sophisticated European socialites, women who had understood he wasn't looking for a relationship that would continue outside the bedroom. Perhaps he could have been forgiven for believing that a tough-talking ex-RAF pilot knew the score. But he had glimpsed Lexi's vulnerability and heard the hurt in her voice when she had explained how, as a child, she had overheard her adoptive parents say that they wished they had not adopted her.

He was jerked from his thoughts by the *whump-whump* of rotor blades. Dragging himself to his feet, he stepped outside the tent and stared up at the helicopter hovering in the blue sky. *What was Lexi playing at?* He watched her fly a circuit of the island before the chopper dipped below the tops of the palm trees.

The rotor blades had almost stopped spinning when Kadir reached the beach. Lexi jumped down from the chopper onto the sand and watched him walk towards her. He had changed back into his royal robes, and in the breeze his white *keffiyeh* fluttered around his tanned face. His dark eyes were no longer warm but hard and unreadable, and with every step he took closer to her she sensed a widening distance between them.

'Why did you take off without me?'

She shrugged. 'I wanted to make a test flight on my own. Although I'd checked underneath the chopper and didn't find an explosive device, I couldn't be certain that the kidnapper hadn't tampered with the controls before he left us stranded here yesterday.'

Kadir was aware of a curious sensation in his chest, as if a fist was gripping his heart. 'Are you saying you flew the helicopter to check it was safe? What if the kidnapper *had* done something to it that caused it to crash? It's very likely you would have been killed.' His jaw clenched. 'You are the craziest woman I've ever met. You should have waited for me instead of risking your life.'

'It is my duty as a pilot to ensure the safety of my aircraft.' Lexi looked at him steadily. 'Your life is more important than mine. You are the Sultan of Zenhab and your people need you to rule the kingdom and build hospitals and universities and continue the work your father started to maintain peace.'

'Of course your life is as valuable as mine, you little idiot,' Kadir said harshly. He was beginning to realise how much harm her adoptive parents had done by failing to make Lexi feel loved and valued. He frowned as the full implication of what she had just said sank in. The possibility that the kidnapper might have placed explosives on the helicopter hadn't occurred to him, but now he visualised the chopper exploding with Lexi on board and imagined her lying lifeless amid the tangled wreckage of the helicopter.

He stared at her. Wearing army-issue combat trousers, a baseball cap and an attitude, she was beautiful and sexy, brave as a lioness yet vulnerable as a day-old kitten.

She'd been vulnerable in his arms last night as they'd made love over and over and—

Was it possible that she was pregnant with his child?

She had told him in Italy that she wasn't on the Pill, but when he had made love to her last night he hadn't given contraception a thought. He had been too swept up with his selfish need for her to think logically, he acknowledged grimly.

Feeling as though he had been struck by a lightning bolt, Kadir realised that *everything* had changed and nothing could continue as he had planned. He was bound by his duty to his kingdom and the promise he had given his father. But if Lexi had conceived his heir, then his greatest duty was to his unborn child.

The grey mountains of Zenhab were rugged and forbidding, and the Bedouin tribes who lived in some of the most ancient settlements in the world were as hardy as their surroundings.

As Lexi landed the helicopter in the cen-

tral square of the fortress town Sanqirah, a
large crowd of curious onlookers gathered in
front of the market stalls, although most people kept their distance and only a few daring
boys surged forward to stare at the chopper.

Kadir's keen eyes noted that there were
a couple of armed security guards posted
around the square, but he was relieved that
Sheikh Omar did not appear to be mustering
his forces, which perhaps meant that Jamal's
plan to incite the tribes into civil unrest had
not yet happened. However, Kadir was aware
that the situation could become more volatile
after he had discussed his marriage contract
to Princess Haleema with her brother.

He jumped out of the helicopter after his
bodyguard Nasim, and spoke to Lexi while
she was sitting in the cockpit. 'I want you to
fly straight back to the palace. I don't know
how long my visit will last, but when I return
we will need to talk.'

What was there to talk about? Lexi wondered
bleakly. Kadir had made it obvious that he was
not going to refer to the fact that they had slept
together. Presumably he regarded their stolen
night of passion as a shameful secret, just as
her birth mother regarded Lexi as a shameful
secret. Her old feelings of insecurity returned.
She had not been good enough for her adoptive

parents or Steven, and now she was not good enough for Kadir. How could she have thought that he might want her when he was about to meet the Princess he was going to marry?

She watched him walk across the courtyard towards Sheikh Omar's palace, his robes billowing behind him. He was a regal, remote Sultan, but she pictured him on Jinan wearing a pair of frayed denim shorts, or wearing nothing but a wickedly sensual smile, and her heart ached.

Sheikh Omar was a young man, and the responsibility of leading the mountain tribes which had been thrust on him after the death of his father, Sheikh Rashid, two months ago showed on his tense face as he greeted the Sultan of Zenhab. Once the servants had poured cups of rich black coffee and placed a plate of sweetmeats on the low table, Omar dismissed his staff so that he and Kadir were alone.

'Welcome to my home, Your Highness.'

'I apologise that my arrival was delayed,' Kadir replied. 'I understand that my uncle Jamal visited you.'

Omar nodded. 'I will speak frankly. Your uncle wishes me to lead the mountain tribes into civil war against you.'

'I know Jamal wants to seize back the Crown

and rule Zenhab. Ten years ago he brokered a marriage arrangement between me and your sister, Princess Haleema, because he believed that with the support of your father he would have more power over me and be able to influence my decisions.' Kadir hesitated. He knew what he must do. His duty lay with Lexi, who might be carrying his child, but as he pictured his father's beloved face his heart ached with remorse. *Forgive me, Baba*, he begged silently.

'My greatest wish is for there to continue to be peace in the kingdom,' he told Omar. 'But I must be honest and tell you that I am unable to honour my marriage contract with Haleema. I intend to outlaw forced marriages, and this is one of many changes which I hope will allow all of the population of Zenhab, men and women, to live their lives with greater freedom.'

In the silence that followed, Kadir was aware of each painful beat of his heart. Would his decision lead Zenhab towards civil disturbance? He knew he was taking a great risk. Ten years ago, when he had sought to claim his right to rule the kingdom, he had been forced by his uncle to sign the marriage agreement with a girl he had never met. But he was no longer prepared to be swayed by threats. He was convinced that forced marriages were wrong, not just in his case, but for the whole population. He was determined to stand up for his beliefs, but he had no idea what the new leader of the mountain tribes thought. The old Sheikh Rashid had been a warmonger, much like Jamal. Was his son any different?

Omar stood up and walked across the room to open a door. When he returned to Kadir he was accompanied by a young woman wearing traditional robes and a headscarf. Her expression was calm and intelligent, and her dark eyes observed Kadir with curiosity.

'This is my sister, Princess Haleema,' Omar introduced her.

'I am pleased to meet you after so many years of wondering about you, and I am even more pleased that you do not wish to marry me, Your Highness,' Haleema said with an unexpected frankness that brought a smile to Kadir's lips.

'Haleema and I share your wish that the peace and prosperity which Zenhab has enjoyed under your rule and, before you, your father, Sultan Khalif, will continue,' Omar said quietly. 'We also share your views on forced marriages. My father told my sister when she was just eleven years old that her marriage had been arranged and she would not be allowed to choose her husband. Haleema wishes to go to university and train to be a doctor, and she has my support. It was not possible when my father was alive. He believed in the old ways and would not have understood my sister's ambition to follow a career, a vocation, which will allow her to help the people in our remote part of Zenhab. But my father is dead and I am the new leader of the mountain tribes.' Omar smiled ruefully. 'Your uncle Jamal was not pleased when I told him that I fully support your rule, Your Highness. I ordered my staff to lock him in his rooms, but I am afraid he managed to escape.'

'I'll issue a warrant for his arrest and have security staff at the airports and ports watch out for him. Jamal cannot be allowed to go free after what he has done.' Kadir's jaw clenched as he remembered those moments on the helicopter when the kidnapper had threatened Lexi with a gun.

In the aftermath of being kidnapped, when they had feared for their lives, it was perhaps unsurprising that their desire for one another, which they had tried so hard to suppress, had finally exploded in fierce passion. With his arranged marriage ended, he had resolved one problem only to face a new one, Kadir brooded, thinking of the possibility that Lexi might be pregnant.

CHAPTER TEN

KADIR COULD NOT fail to notice Lexi's suitcase standing in the middle of the sitting room when he followed her into her apartment at the palace. She had refused to meet his gaze when she'd opened the door, and he could feel the tension emanating from her slender frame as she stood on the opposite side of the room from him.

'Are you going somewhere?' he murmured.

'I'm going back to England. You agreed to release me from my contract after I had flown you to the mountains to visit Haleema,' she reminded him.

'The situation has changed. I agreed to you leaving before we became lovers.'

'We are not lovers!' She whirled round to face him, her blue eyes flashing. 'We spent one night together but we shouldn't have done. We should both have been stronger and not given in to desire.'

Lexi turned away from Kadir and cursed her

traitorous heart for leaping when she sensed him walk across the room towards her. The familiar scent of his aftershave stole around her and she dared not look at his handsome face. The moment she had opened the door and seen him, dressed in black jeans and a polo shirt, she had struggled to maintain her composure. She wished she had left the palace before he'd returned, as she had originally planned to do. But she could not leave Zenhab without saying goodbye.

'I think it was inevitable that we would make love.' His deep voice broke into her thoughts. 'We were attracted to each other from the moment we first met.'

How could he sound so matter-of-fact about the most incredible night of her life? Perhaps because for him it had just been sex, Lexi thought bleakly. And, having satisfied his inconvenient desire for her, he had hurried to meet his future bride.

'I take it that you met Haleema? So, when is the wedding?'

Kadir heard the hurt in her voice and guilt washed over him because he knew he was to blame. Lexi might be acting like a spitting wildcat, but he had discovered on Jinan that she was so vulnerable.

'I did meet her and her brother. I told them

that I wished to break the marriage arrangement, and Haleema and Omar supported my decision.'

'You broke your marriage contract!' Lexi's heart gave another painful lurch. 'But I thought you had to marry Haleema in order to keep peace and avoid civil war.'

'That was true when Sheikh Rashid was alive. My uncle Jamal could count on Rashid's support. But Omar is not like his father. He wants peace in the kingdom and welcomes changes to some of the old traditions.'

'So Jamal's plan to cause trouble backfired.'

'Yes, thankfully. My uncle is now in custody after he was arrested trying to leave the country.'

Lexi shivered as she remembered those terrifying moments when she had feared that the kidnapper might kill them. On the island her emotions had been raw, and she had been unable to resist Kadir because facing death had forced her to face up to the truth—that she was halfway to falling in love with him.

But even though he had ended his marriage arrangement with Haleema, she had no expectation that he wanted a relationship with *her*.

She picked up an envelope from the table and thrust it at him. 'It's my letter of resignation. You agreed to forget the financial penalty if I end my contract early, but if you've changed your mind I'll send you the money I owe when I'm back in England.'

Kadir opened the letter and skimmed his eyes over the terse two lines Lexi had written. 'How will you repay me when you have other debts?'

She stiffened. 'How do you know about my private life?'

'You know I had a detailed security check run on you before I employed you as my helicopter pilot.'

'It's a pity you didn't run a more detailed check on Fariq. It would have saved a lot of trouble.' If they hadn't been kidnapped and stranded on Jinan, their heightened emotions wouldn't have exploded in frantic passion and they would not have made love.

Lexi grimaced. Love hadn't been involved. They'd had sex, and just because it had been amazing, mind-blowing sex she had stupidly hoped that she meant something to Kadir. But the truth was she meant nothing to him and now that he was free from his arranged marriage he could choose who he wanted to marry. No doubt he would want a beautiful socialite to be his bride, she thought dully. In England he was Earl Montgomery and one of the most eligible bachelors in Europe.

Kadir slipped the letter into his pocket. 'The financial penalty clause in your contract does not apply because it is not your fault that you have to resign.' Kadir paused and took a deep breath before taking a step towards Lexi. 'Have you considered the possibility that you could be pregnant?'

Lexi's eyes widened.

'The Civil Aviation Authority's advice to female pilots is that they should not fly in the early stages of pregnancy,' Kadir continued.

Lexi bit her lip, wondering how he could sound so calm about something so potentially life-changing. But if she *was* pregnant it was not his life that would change, she thought grimly.

'It's unlikely I'm pregnant. It was the wrong time of the month for me to have conceived.'

He gave her an impatient look. 'We both know that can't be predicted. We will need to know for sure.'

'Well, since I'm boringly regular, I'll tell you in just over a week.' She hated herself for blushing, thinking how ridiculous it was to feel embarrassed about discussing such a personal issue when Kadir had seen, touched and kissed every centimetre of her body. 'I'm certain there's nothing to worry about, but if there are any repercussions from our irresponsible behaviour I'll let you know,' she told him with a forced airiness.

The situation felt surreal. She *couldn't* be carrying Kadir's baby, Lexi assured herself. But the stark fact was that pregnancy *was* a possibility after she'd had unprotected sex. Actually, she felt a bit sick, but she was probably imagining it, she told herself. What she definitely felt was a fool. She was a sensible, responsible twenty-nine-year-old and she had no excuse for risking an unplanned pregnancy. But when Kadir had stripped her naked in the tent on Jinan her only thought been how desperately she wanted him to hold her, to feel safe in his arms and for him to make love to her.

She picked up her suitcase and opened the drawer in the bureau to retrieve her passport. 'I'll phone you from England once I have any news.'

'If you are pregnant you will marry me.'

Her head whipped round, and the fact that the drawer was empty did not register in her brain at first. 'Don't be ridiculous.'

'You have a better suggestion?'

He was serious? Lexi laughed shakily. '*If* I'm pregnant, which I am quite sure I'm not because I can't believe fate would play such a ghastly joke, then it will be my problem and I'll deal with it.'

He swore. 'If by *deal with it* you mean what I think you mean...'

Something in his voice, an indefinable emotion, made her pause, and she paled as *his* meaning sank into her dazed mind. 'I would never do that.' Shocked beyond words, her hand shot out before she had time to think and she struck his cheek, leaving a red imprint of her fingers on his olive skin.

His eyes glittered dangerously and he caught hold of her arm as if he thought she might slap him again. But Lexi was horrified by her loss of control and her mouth trembled, betraying her intense hurt.

'My biological mother admitted that she wanted to abort me,' she said thickly, 'but by the time she found out it was too late to get rid of me.' She swallowed. 'If it turns out that I have conceived your child I will take care of it and...and *love* it, because I know better than most what it's like for a child not to feel loved.'

'And I know what it feels like for a child to *be* loved.' Kadir's dark eyes burned into hers. 'My father showered me with love and affection, and I have every intention of doing the same with my child. The baby that is possibly already developing inside you will be my heir, and if you are carrying my son he will be the future Sultan of Zenhab. But, more important, our child has the right to be brought up by both its parents. Far from being ridiculous, marriage is the only option I will consider.'

Lexi felt as if an iron band was squeezing her lungs. Kadir's words and, even more, the fierce emotion in them, filled her with a strange sense of relief that if the unthinkable had happened and she was actually pregnant, he would accept responsibility for his child.

He would be a wonderful father, she thought. In her mind she pictured a baby with olive-gold skin and dark curls and thick black eyelashes. She imagined Kadir cradling his son in his arms and she felt a sudden acute longing to be part of the tableaux, for Kadir to look at her with the same love in his eyes that he felt for his child.

What was she thinking? 'There are other ways that we could both be parents to our child without a sham marriage that neither of us wants,' she said stiffly.

'Not in Zenhab there aren't. The kingdom is becoming more progressive, but the Zenhabian people will not tolerate their Sultan fathering an illegitimate child.'

Kadir suddenly smiled and the sexy curl of his lips evoked a purely physical longing in the pit of Lexi's stomach. 'If we have to marry, it won't be a sham, certainly not in the bedroom. I already have proof that we are sexually compatible.'

Lexi saw determination stamped on his hard-boned features and panic gripped her. He was deadly serious that if she was pregnant he would insist on them marrying for the sake of their child. He had been freed from his arranged marriage, only to be faced with a marriage of convenience and she would be his unwanted wife, just as she had been her adoptive parents' unwanted daughter once they'd had a daughter of their own.

'I doubt the Zenhabian people would support a marriage between us if they knew the circumstances of my birth,' she said tautly. She had never revealed to anyone the truth of her background, but once Kadir learned the facts she was sure he would drop the crazy marriage idea. 'And they *would* find out about me. Your press may not be as intrusive as the European paparazzi, but someone will dig up the dirt about me.'

His eyes narrowed. 'What do you mean?'

'A woman named Cathy Barnes is my biological mother. During the early years of her life she worked as a prostitute, selling sex to fund her drug habit. My father was...' she shrugged helplessly '...one of her clients, a stranger who went to a hotel room and paid for sex with a woman he would never see again, much less know that his sordid transaction had resulted in a child. Me.'

'You told me you knew nothing about your real parents.'

'My background is hardly something to be proud of,' she said drily. She sighed. 'Like many adopted children, I imagine, I was curious about who had brought me into the world and, without any facts to go on, I created a fantasy that my real parents had been forced by tragic circumstances to give me away, but they had always loved me and were desperate for us to be reunited.'

The unconsciously wistful note in her voice evoked a pang of sympathy in Kadir but he knew she would hate any suggestion of pity. He strolled across to the window overlooking the palace courtyard where the helicopter was parked on the pad.

He remembered the night his yacht had capsized off the south coast of England and his relief when he had looked up and seen the coastguard helicopter piloted by Lexi which had come to his rescue. It was due to her fearlessness that his life had been saved. And she had demonstrated her bravery again when she had calmly flown the helicopter while the kidnapper had stuck a gun in her ribs. But, beneath her tough exterior, Kadir knew she hid a vulnerability that touched something inside him.

'How did you learn the truth about your biological mother?'

'When I was eighteen the adoption agency helped me to trace her. But my hope that I would feel an instant bond with her was quickly shattered. Cathy agreed to meet me, but there was no emotional reunion,' Lexi said wryly. 'She told me that she hadn't wanted a baby and had handed me to a social worker immediately after I was born. When I finally met Cathy, she had sorted her life out and was married, but her husband had no idea of her past life or that she'd had a child and, because she is ashamed of her past, she has never told anyone about me.'

'Do you keep in contact with her?'

'We meet a few times a year, always in secret,' Lexi said bitterly. 'Six months ago Cathy learned that she has cancer which is untreatable. She broke down when she told me that she had built up huge debts on credit cards that her husband did not know about. She knew he would be worried about the money she owed and she was upset that their last few months together would be spoiled, so I offered to pay the debts for her.'

'It was good of you to help her when she doesn't seem to have been much of a mother to you.'

'She's my mother,' Lexi said flatly. 'She was in a desperate situation when she gave birth to me, and I think she tried to do her best for me by having me adopted. Surely you can understand now, why, even if I am pregnant, you can't marry me. The Zenhabian people were expecting you to marry a princess and I doubt they would accept a whore's daughter for their Sultana.'

Kadir caught hold of her chin when she looked away from him as if she was embarrassed to meet his gaze. 'Lexi, whatever your mother was and however she lived her life has no bearing on who you are. No one could fail to be impressed by your courage and your compassion. If you are pregnant I can't think of anyone who would be a better mother to my child, and as my wife you would be a great role model to young women in Zenhab.'

Lexi swallowed. He sounded as if he meant what he had said, but a voice of caution inside her head warned her that she would be a fool to trust him. The truth was that if she had conceived Kadir's baby he was prepared to marry her *only* because he wanted his child.

She dragged her eyes from the molten

warmth in his and spun away from him. 'This conversation is premature and almost certainly pointless. I'm sure I'm not pregnant. There's a flight leaving Zenhab for Dubai, from there I can catch a direct flight back to London, and I intend to be on it.'

She stared at the empty drawer in the bureau. 'I know I put my passport in here.' She suddenly remembered that the maid who cleaned her apartment had opened the drawer and quickly shut it again when Lexi had entered the room earlier. 'One of the staff wouldn't have taken it, would they?'

'Yes, on my instruction,' Kadir said coolly. 'But don't worry. I have it safely locked away in my study and if you are not pregnant I'll return it to you.'

Her shock turned swiftly to fury. 'You *stole* my passport?'

'Borrowed,' he drawled.

'That's *outrageous*. How *dare* you? I *demand* you return it immediately.' Lexi could feel her blood pounding through her veins, but her anger was mixed with apprehension when she realised that she was effectively a prisoner in Zenhab and probably at the palace, she thought, remembering the guards who protected the perimeter walls and gates. Kadir could not force her to marry him, she reminded herself.

As if he could read her mind, he said inexorably, 'If the news is positive, we will marry without delay before word gets out that you are carrying the Sultan's child.'

Kadir's jaw hardened. Taking Lexi's passport had been a panic reaction to prevent her from leaving, and he acknowledged that she had every right to be angry. But if she left she might refuse to return to Zenhab. And if she was pregnant she might decide to bring up her child—*his* child—on her own in England. He knew she was fiercely independent, and it was possible that she wouldn't want to spend her life in a remote desert kingdom.

He remembered how his mother had hated Zenhab and the restrictions of being the wife of the Sultan. Judith Montgomery had abandoned her husband and seven-year-old son to live at the Montgomery estate in Windsor, but whenever Kadir had visited his mother she had put emotional pressure on him to live in England with her.

Kadir grimaced as he remembered his mother's tears when he'd said goodbye to her at the end of each visit. He had loved both his parents and had felt torn between them. His mother had made him feel guilty for choosing to live with his father and he had spent his childhood shuttling back and forth between his parents and the two very different cultures in Zenhab and England.

If Lexi was pregnant, he would not want his child to go through what he had as a child, to feel torn loyalties and guilt, as he had done. Somehow he must try to convince Lexi that their child, if there was a child, deserved to be brought up by both of them in a stable family unit. But he could not abandon his duty to his kingdom. He was a Sultan and his child would be heir to the throne. Marriage to Lexi was the only option.

But what if, after a few years of marriage, she left him like his mother had left his father? How would he feel if she decided that life in the desert kingdom was not for her? Sultan Khalif had been heartbroken by his wife's desertion, Kadir remembered. As a teenager, he had watched his father sitting alone in the gardens that had been created for Judith, and he had vowed that he would never lose his heart to a woman. Love had been his strong father's one weakness, but Kadir knew better than to risk his emotions on something as unreliable as love.

Lexi stared at Kadir's chiselled features and wondered what he was thinking. He had insisted that if she was pregnant he would marry her, and she supposed she should feel relieved that her child would have a father. But the harsh truth was that his child was all he was interested in. He had proved that he was not interested in her when he had virtually ignored her after the night they had spent together on Jinan.

She tried to hold on to her anger. She needed to be strong to stand up to him and not allow him to push her into a loveless marriage that would be convenient for him but heartbreaking for her. But her fire and her temper had deserted her and she felt empty and alone, just as she had been all her life. No one had really wanted her or loved her, she thought bleakly. Memories of her childhood, when she had been made to feel a nuisance by her adoptive parents, still hurt. How could she marry Kadir, knowing that he did not want her—apart from for sex? she thought, remembering how he had said that they were sexually compatible.

'I wish none of this had happened,' she said in a choked voice.

An odd expression flared in Kadir's eyes. 'Do you regret making love with me?'

How could she regret the most beautiful night of her life? 'Do you?' she countered.

'No.' The night they had spent together on

the island had been magical—a stolen night of pleasure when he had been able to forget the responsibilities of being a Sultan.

The molten warmth in Kadir's eyes sent a warning shiver through Lexi. She dared not soften towards him. When had he moved closer to her? The heat of his body and the evocative masculine scent of him tugged on her senses. If he touched her she would be lost! Suddenly scared of what she might reveal, Lexi tried to twist away from him, but he settled his hands on her shoulders and pulled her to him.

His body was all hard muscle and sinew, and the feel of his erection nudging her thigh made her insides melt.

'I will never regret the pleasure and the passion we shared on Jinan,' he said softly.

'Don't...' she pleaded as she watched his head descend. She struggled against the strength of his arms holding her, but her real battle was with herself and her body betrayed her the moment he claimed her lips and kissed her with the ruthless mastery of a desert warrior.

It was sweet rapture to be in his arms, to lay her hand on his chest and feel the erratic thud of his heart, to know that his arousal was as swift and all-consuming as her own. She had thought he would never kiss her again, that their stolen night was all she would ever have of him. She had no protection against his sorcery, no defence against the bone-shaking tenderness of his kiss as he eased the pressure of his mouth on hers and traced the swollen contours of her lips with the tip of his tongue.

'Do you still doubt we could make our marriage work?'

Lexi swept her lashes down to blot out the satisfied gleam in Kadir's eyes. Of course he looked triumphant when she had capitulated so utterly and responded to him so shamelessly, she thought bleakly. Her mouth was stinging from his hungry passion, and she told herself she must have imagined an underlying tenderness in his kiss that had tugged on her frayed emotions.

'It's just sex,' she muttered. 'I don't deny the chemistry that ignites whenever we're within a few feet of each other, but it's not a basis for marriage.'

She assumed he would step away from her, and was unprepared when he framed her face in his hands and murmured, 'Was it *just sex* we had on Jinan? I have never experienced such intense pleasure as when we made love, and I can't help feeling that we shared something more than merely physical satiation.'

On the island Kadir had tried to dismiss the

surprising feelings that had swept over him in the languorous aftermath of making love to Lexi. He had been aware that he could not allow himself to feel anything because he was bound by duty to honour his arranged marriage. But since he had ended his marriage arrangement with Haleema he could not stop thinking about the sex with Lexi, which had been amazing. But he also remembered that when she had fallen asleep in his arms he had remained awake to protect her if the kidnapper returned; he had held her close to him and studied how her long eyelashes curled against her cheeks.

'You're just saying that because if it turns out that I am pregnant you want me to stay in Zenhab so that you can be a father to your child.'

Kadir saw the mistrust in her eyes and understood it all the more now that she had told him how her biological mother had rejected her.

'I don't deny I would want custody of my child,' he admitted, determined to be honest with her. 'I would be prepared to seek a legal ruling if necessary.'

He wanted much more, he acknowledged. He had told Lexi once that he wanted everything, and he knew with sudden insight that it was true.

She paled. 'Do you mean you would fight for custody if I have a baby?'

For the first time since the nightmare had begun, Lexi considered the real possibility that she was pregnant. Supposing she had a baby, a tiny, vulnerable scrap of life, utterly dependent on her, that she could love and who would love her unconditionally? Unconsciously, she placed her hand over her stomach, the instinct of maternal protectiveness kicking inside her.

'I would *never* give up my child. I've told you how my birth mother gave me away. How could you think I would do the same?'

The glimmer of tears in her eyes got to Kadir. 'I know you wouldn't,' he said roughly. 'So I suggest we stop the talk of fighting and custody and spend the next week or so getting to know each other better because, if you are carrying our child, then, like it or not, we will be spending the foreseeable future together.'

His suggestion of calling a truce made sense, Lexi acknowledged reluctantly. Nothing would persuade her to give up her child. Even if she managed to leave the palace and return to England, Kadir would find out if she was pregnant and he would use his wealth and power to claim his heir. In a strange way she was glad of his determination to be a devoted father, unlike the faceless man who had accidentally fathered her.

He took her silence as agreement. 'We'll start by having dinner tonight. Unfortunately, we won't be alone because Yusuf reminded me that the French ambassador is coming to dinner at the palace this evening, but it will be good practice for you if you become Sultana of Zenhab.'

She did not return his smile. 'The idea is laughable, isn't it?' she said in a low voice full of self-doubt, 'considering my genes. I don't know how to talk to an ambassador.'

'Just be you,' Kadir advised. He glanced at his watch. 'I'm expecting a phone call. Dinner will be at eight.' On his way out of the door, he glanced back at her. 'I've taken the liberty of ordering some clothes for you. I will be hosting several social functions over the coming week and you'll need evening dresses,' he explained quickly when he saw the battle gleam in her eyes.

'I don't want you to pay for my clothes...' Lexi stared at the door as Kadir closed it after him. The snick of the catch made her feel trapped; although he had not locked her in her apartment and presumably she could walk around the palace and gardens, she was not at liberty to leave the kingdom—at least, not until they knew if she was pregnant or not.

If she *hadn't* conceived his child then, no doubt, she would find herself on the next flight out of Zenhab, and Kadir would be free to marry a woman of his choice.

She bit her lip and pushed away the crazy idea that she secretly hoped she was pregnant. She had spent her whole life hoping to find love, but she knew with painful certainty that her heart's desire would not be granted here in the Sultan's palace.

The evening was less of an ordeal than she had expected. The French ambassador had been invited to the palace, ostensibly to discuss opportunities for business investment in Zenhab but, with typical Gallic charm, he flirted with Lexi throughout dinner so that she soon relaxed and chatted away to him, earning her several hard stares from Kadir. Until her possible pregnancy was confirmed he had no right to look at her with brooding possessiveness in his eyes that in the flickering candlelight were the colour of bitter chocolate, she thought indignantly.

But once again the devil inside her enjoyed goading him, and she could not deny a sense of satisfaction when she met his gaze across the table and watched streaks of colour flare along his cheekbones. He might not love her, but he desired her.

She was glad she had abandoned her pride and worn one of the dresses that had been delivered to her apartment. The full-length black velvet gown had a modest neckline, in respect for Zenhabian culture, but it was expertly designed to show off her slim waist, and the colour was a perfect foil for her pale blonde hair that she had left loose so that it fell smooth and sleek to halfway down her back.

Kadir walked beside her as the party moved from the dining room outside to the terrace, where coffee was to be served. 'I commend your efforts to encourage Zenhabian-French relations,' he said curtly, 'but I would prefer you not to flirt with Monsieur Aubrech.'

Lexi gave him an impatient look. 'I was simply being friendly, and I have to say it wouldn't have hurt you to have been a bit more amenable during dinner instead of scowling at Etienne. What's wrong with you tonight?'

Where did he start? He had never experienced jealousy before, but every time Lexi had laughed at one of the ambassador's jokes Kadir had felt corrosive acid fizzing in the pit of his stomach, and he had spent the entire dinner fighting the urge to ignore social niceties and carry her off to have hot, hard sex with her on the nearest available flat surface.

Aware that he was scowling as she had accused him of doing, he muttered something about her pushing his patience and strode onto the terrace, determined to keep the over-friendly French ambassador away from Lexi.

At the end of the evening, Lexi's temper was still simmering over Kadir's unfair accusation that she had been flirting with the French ambassador. She walked into her bedroom and smiled as she dismissed the maid who had turned down the sheets on her bed. Picking up her hairbrush from the dressing table, she heard a faint sound behind her and whirled around with a startled cry as the bathroom door opened and Kadir appeared.

'What are…?' She broke off when he put a finger to his lips, warning her to be quiet.

'Has the maid gone?' he murmured. 'Go and lock your bedroom door.'

She marched across the room and turned the key in the lock before she turned to face him, and immediately wished she hadn't when she realised he was naked apart from a towel knotted dangerously low on his hips. He was rubbing his damp hair with another towel. Lexi forced her eyes up from his naked, bronzed chest to his face and felt her stomach dip as she studied the sensual curve of his mouth and the sexy stubble that covered his jaw.

'Why didn't you want the maid to see you?'

He shrugged. 'It's better not to publicly advertise our relationship just yet, at least until we know if you are pregnant. It is against Zenhabian custom for men and women to share a bedroom before marriage.'

'So instead you are skulking around the palace and visiting me in secret.' She welcomed her temper to disguise her hurt that once again she was a shameful secret. 'I have no intention of sharing my bedroom with you,' Lexi told him furiously. 'You said we should spend time getting to know one another better, but you obviously thought I would provide ten nights of sex. I don't suppose I'll even see you in the daytime.'

'On the contrary; I've arranged for us to spend tomorrow at the coast. I thought you might like to learn to sail my yacht, and we could anchor in a secluded little bay I know of and swim or even snorkel. There are some beautiful fish and the water is crystal-clear.'

'Oh…well, I guess that does sound fun.' She bit her lip, unable to drag her eyes from the sensual gleam in his, and her heart suddenly began to hammer. 'But that doesn't explain why you are here.'

'Why do you think?' he said softly.

The dangerous glitter in his eyes as he walked towards her had her hurriedly backing up against the door.

'I don't want to sleep with you.' She was aware that now he was free from his marriage contract there was nothing to stop them being lovers, but she did not dare have sex with him again. Not now she had revealed intensely personal things about herself and her background that she had never told anyone else. She had made herself emotionally vulnerable to Kadir. Damn it, she had fallen in love with him. But he did not love her, and she did not trust herself to make love with him without giving away how she felt about him.

'That's okay because sleep is the last thing I had in mind, too.' Lexi's spine was jammed against the door and Kadir trapped her there by placing his hands on either side of her head so that his body was almost touching hers. 'Shall I tell you what *is* in my mind, *habibi*?'

'Don't...call me that.' She turned her head so that he wouldn't see the tears that stung her eyes. Her emotions were see-sawing all over the place. Perhaps it was a sign she was pregnant? Distracted by the mental picture of holding her baby in her arms, she had no time to defend her heart against the sweet seduction of Kadir's mouth as he claimed her lips in a kiss that stirred her soul.

'I want you to trust me. I don't want to hurt you, Lexi,' he said softly.

But he would, she thought with a flash of despair. If she was carrying his baby he would insist on marrying her, but she would be his unwanted wife, and if she wasn't pregnant, his desire for her would fade as quickly as it had with his other mistresses.

Her brain urged her to resist his sensual foreplay, but he had lowered her zip and tugged the top of her dress down, baring her to his hungry gaze. His hands were exquisitely gentle as he cupped her breasts in his palms and rubbed his thumb pads over her nipples until they hardened and tingled and the pleasure was too intense for her to bear.

'Let me love you,' he said in his deep, dark voice that wrapped around her like a velvet cloak. She knew he meant *make love to you*, and she knew she would be a fool to succumb to his sorcery. But for the next few days and nights he would be hers, whispered a voice inside her head. Her future was on hold until she found out if she was pregnant so why not enjoy what he was offering now?

Anticipation licked like scorching flames through her as he swept her up in his arms and carried her over to the bed. Entranced by the magic he was summoning with his mouth and hands, she had no recollection of him removing her dress and knickers, and she was unaware of the savage kick of desire Kadir felt in his gut as he stared at the erotic contrast of her ash-blonde hair and creamy pale limbs spread against the black silk sheets.

Spread for his pleasure, Kadir thought as he pushed her legs apart and knelt above her. He had never known any other woman to be as responsive and generous a lover as Lexi, and he had never felt such powerful thunder in his heart as he felt with her. He wanted everything, he acknowledged. And the desert king always took what he desired.

CHAPTER ELEVEN

'WELL—ANY NEWS?' Kadir demanded the moment Lexi emerged from the en suite bathroom.

'Nothing yet,' she murmured. She slid back into bed and Kadir curled his arm around her and drew her into the warmth of his body. His spicy cologne teased her senses and the whorls of black hairs on his chest tickled her cheek. These moments in the early morning when they lay together, half dozing, muscles aching pleasurably after long hours of lovemaking the previous night, were dangerously intoxicating, she thought ruefully as she snuggled up to him.

'You're late.'

'It's not an exact science,' she said drily. But actually her monthly cycle was as regular as clockwork. Lexi felt a heart-thumping mixture of dread and excitement. She had never been even one day late before. She might be imagining it, but she was sure her breasts looked a bit fuller when she'd glanced in the bathroom mirror.

She couldn't be pregnant, she assured herself. And of *course* she did not want to be. She could never forget that she had been an accidental pregnancy, unwanted by her mother. It shamed her that she had made one stupid mistake and it would be better for everyone if there were no consequences.

She bit her lip as Kadir placed his hand on her flat stomach. What if his baby was inside her? For years she had been absorbed in her career and had never really had any maternal feelings. But when she had left the RAF, and with her thirtieth birthday on the horizon, she'd begun to feel wistful whenever she held one of her friends' newborn infants. For the past eleven days she had found herself scrutinising every tiny symptom that might mean she was going to be a mother.

'You had better do a test. And if it confirms what we both suspect I'll start making arrangements for our wedding.' Kadir rolled onto his back, taking Lexi with him, and slid his hand into her hair, urging her mouth down onto his. The kiss was slow and sweet, drugging her senses and stealing her heart as she sensed tenderness in his passion.

The past week and a half had been wonderful, she thought dreamily. Kadir had spent every day with her, only popping into his office briefly to deal with any urgent matters that his chief adviser deemed to require his attention. He had given her sailing lessons on his yacht, and they had swum in a turquoise sea that was as warm as a bath. Lexi enjoyed their trips to different parts of Zenhab, including driving out to the desert in a four-by-four, but, for all Kadir's determination to spend a few carefree days, he was still the Sultan and they were always accompanied by bodyguards. Only within the palace walls were they able to be completely private, and several times he had instructed the staff not to disturb them before making love to her on a sun lounger by the pool.

'What would you like to do today?' His voice was indulgent as he stroked her hair back from her face. 'Perhaps you had better not do anything too energetic in case the pregnancy test is positive.'

Kadir was growing increasingly convinced that Lexi had conceived his baby. The very real possibility that he was going to be a father made him miss his own father, and he wished Sultan Khalif could have seen his grandchild. Thoughts of fatherhood had also brought back memories of his childhood, when he had felt torn between his parents, and he was more determined than ever to persuade Lexi that they should marry and stay together for the sake of their child.

He traced his hands over her slender figure and imagined her belly swollen with his baby. Skimming lower, he began to stroke her buttocks in rhythmic circles. 'We could spend the day in bed?'

'I thought you said I shouldn't do anything too energetic,' she said breathlessly, instantly turned on by the sensuous motion of Kadir's hand caressing her bottom.

He gave a wickedly sexy smile as he flipped her onto her back. 'You won't have to do anything. I'll do all the work and you can just lie back and enjoy me pleasuring you.'

Oh, God! She curled her fingers into the silk sheet as he kissed his way down her body from her breasts to the sweet spot between her thighs and flicked his tongue over her clitoris until she moaned and pressed her feminine heat against his mouth. He took her with his tongue and then drove his rock-hard arousal deep inside her and took her to the peak again so that her first orgasm had barely ended when the next one began.

His passion seemed wilder, more uncontrolled, and when he came the cords on his neck stood out and he groaned her name as if it had been torn from his soul. Overwhelmed by the feelings that overspilled her heart, Lexi wrapped her arms around him and hugged him tightly, uncaring at that moment that her tender smile betrayed her.

'You know I have to leave tomorrow, and I'll be away for a week?' he said later when they had showered together and were eating a very late breakfast on the balcony. 'Sheikh Omar has organised meetings with the mountain tribes; I am hoping I can persuade them to swear their allegiance to the Crown.'

Kadir looked across the table at Lexi and thought that she had never looked more beautiful, with her long blonde hair falling around her shoulders and her bright blue eyes sparkling like precious gems. She seemed softer somehow, and he had noticed a dreamy expression in her eyes that made him wonder if his patience was paying off and she was beginning to trust him.

The rest of the day and night passed too quickly, and Lexi sensed an urgency in Kadir's caresses when he made love to her in the cool grey light of dawn, before he slid out of bed and headed into his dressing room to prepare for his trip to the northern territories. He emerged dressed in his robes of state, his *keffiyeh* held in place on his head by a circle of gold.

'I've left a pregnancy test kit in the bathroom. Try to call me if you have any news, but communication in the mountains is limited—something I will be working with Omar to improve in the future.' He dropped a brief fierce kiss on her mouth. 'I wish I didn't have to go,' he groaned. 'Why don't you do the test now?'

Butterflies leapt in Lexi's stomach. What if the pregnancy test gave a positive result? *What if it didn't?* Either way, her relationship with Kadir would be affected. She suddenly wished the past eleven days could last for ever.

'It will be better to wait a few more days to make sure the test gives a correct result.'

'All right.' He kissed her again, softer this time, his lips clinging to hers as if he really did not want to leave her, almost making her believe that he cared for her a little.

She missed him the second he strode out of the bedroom and closed the door behind him. An inexplicable sadness filled her, a feeling that the days they had spent together had been a golden time that had slipped through her fingers like the desert sand and now had disappeared for ever.

The hours without Kadir dragged, and the

huge bed was a lonely place without him lying next to her.

Next morning, a trip to the bathroom revealed that the niggling stomach ache she'd had during the night was not indigestion as she had thought—as she had hoped, she acknowledged dully.

There seemed no point doing the pregnancy test now she had evidence that she had not conceived Kadir's baby. She ordered herself to feel relieved but her heart disobeyed and an unexpected torrent of grief ripped through her. Faced with reality, she admitted the truth. She would have loved to be a mother, loved to have Kadir's child—loved him, she thought painfully.

She'd felt so close to him recently that she had even started to believe that, if they were going to be parents, perhaps they could have a successful marriage. A few times she had caught Kadir looking at her in a way that had made her heart leap. But now reality brought her crashing back down to earth. He did not love her, and when he learned that she was not expecting his baby he would send her away from Zenhab and search for a suitable bride to be the mother of his heir.

The strident ring of her phone made her jump. She stared at the handset, wondering if

Kadir was calling her. If it was him, shouldn't she break the news that he wasn't going to be a father?

Athena greeted her cheerfully. 'How is everything in Zenhab? I was thinking about you, and I had a funny feeling that something's wrong.'

Lexi forced an airy tone. 'You and your funny feelings!' Actually, she recalled her sister had had a 'feeling' when she had phoned Lexi in Afghanistan the day that her co-pilot had been killed. 'Everything is fine; couldn't be better, in fact.'

Afterwards, she did not know what made her confide in Athena, but she felt more alone than she had felt in her life and her sister's gentle voice reached out to her. The whole story of being kidnapped with Kadir and stranded on his island came tumbling out, along with the fact that she'd had unprotected sex with him, and his insistence that if she was pregnant he would marry her.

'But you're not pregnant,' Athena repeated what Lexi had just told her. 'What a shame. You would be a wonderful mother, and a great wife for the Sultan.'

'Of course it's not a shame,' Lexi said sharply. 'You're such a daydreamer, Athena. The fact that I'm not pregnant is good news.

It means I can carry on with my career. I couldn't be happier...' she choked, and suddenly she couldn't hold back her tears. It was as if a dam had burst and her grief for the baby she had imagined holding in her arms poured out, along with a lifetime of pain and hurt at feeling rejected and unloved. Her secret hope that she would spend the future with Kadir and their child was over, and now she had nothing.

'Why don't you tell Kadir you love him?' Athena asked softly. 'What have you got to lose?'

'Apart from my pride, dignity and self-respect, you mean?' Lexi's chest hurt from crying so hard. She had never lost control of her emotions so violently before and she felt scared that loving Kadir had changed her, weakened her, and she would never be tough-talking, no-nonsense Lexi Howard again.

'I wish I was with you in Zenhab to give you a hug,' her sister said. 'I wish I could help. You know I love you, Lexi.'

Lexi swallowed. She *did* know that Athena cared for her, but she had always struggled to show her own emotions. 'You're a great sister. I...I love you too,' she said huskily.

She sensed Athena's surprise. 'You've never said it before. I think you should tell Kadir how you feel about him and give him a chance to explain why he seems so determined to marry you.'

'It was only because he wanted his child. But there isn't going to be one. He's the Sultan of Zenhab and needs to marry a woman of royal blood, not someone whose genes come from a very murky pool.'

'What will you do?'

'Come home, look for a job.' She still needed to pay off Cathy's debts, Lexi thought wearily. She remembered that Kadir had taken her passport and she would have to stay on at the palace until he returned from his trip to the mountains. It was only fair to tell him her news in person rather than leave a message on his phone.

Memories of the past days they had spent exclusively in each other's company pushed into her mind. Had she imagined that they had had fun together, shared laughter, *friendship*? Could she do what her sister had suggested and tell Kadir she had fallen in love with him?

Her stomach swooped at the idea of risking his rejection. Kadir had only wanted her when he had thought she could be carrying his baby, and the traditions of his kingdom meant he could not allow his child to be born illegitimate, she reminded herself. She was certain he would be relieved not to be forced into a marriage he did not want.

The helicopter buzzed above the palace before dropping down to land in the courtyard. Kadir had hired a new pilot, an Australian guy called Mitch, who Lexi assumed would continue to work for the Sultan after she had gone.

She had carried her suitcase down to the entrance hall and as she watched Kadir walk up the palace steps she pulled the peak of her cap lower over her eyes. The clothes he had bought her were hanging in the wardrobe in the apartment she had first occupied when she had arrived in Zenhab. She had applied for a job in the UK, flying workers out to oil rigs in the North Sea, and she doubted there would be many opportunities to wear designer evening gowns in the cold winter in Aberdeen.

Wearing her pilot's uniform made her feel more like herself. A grey skirt and jacket teamed with a crisp white blouse, and her hair swept up beneath her cap, gave the impression of cool professionalism and hid the truth that her heart was breaking. Through a window, she studied the Sultan in his traditional robes and tried to feel distanced from him, but memories of Kadir, naked, beautiful, lowering his body onto hers, threatened to shatter her composure.

She took a few steps forward as he swept through the great palace doors, halting when his dark eyes immediately shot to her suitcase.

His smile faded. 'Do you have news for me?'

'I'm sure you will be as relieved as I am to hear that I'm not pregnant.' Her jaw ached as she flashed him a brittle smile. 'Our worries were needless, but now we can both get on with our lives.'

Kadir's eyes narrowed and he fought the urge to whip Lexi's damn cap off her head so that he could see her face. She sounded so cool and in control, reminding him of the ice queen who had rescued him from his capsized yacht and ripped into him for risking the lives of his crew.

He absorbed her words. There was to be no child. No son to love, as his father had loved him. No daughter to adore, with silvery-blonde hair and eyes the colour of mountain skies. No requirement under Zenhabian tradition to marry Lexi. She had said she was relieved not to be pregnant. Maybe she was right, he brooded.

'It's probably for the best.' He glanced around the entrance hall, suddenly aware of the presence of several palace staff. Ignoring his chief adviser who was hurrying towards him, he caught hold of Lexi's elbow and steered her into his study, shutting the door and locking it to ensure their privacy.

'Was it necessary to manhandle me?' she complained, rubbing her arm. 'Why have you brought me in here?'

He countered her question with one of his own. 'Why are you leaving?'

'I've told you why. I'm not carrying your baby. You have hired a new pilot so there's no reason for me to stay in Zenhab.' It took all Lexi's will power to keep her voice steady. Kadir had said it was for the best that she wasn't pregnant. Of course he was pleased, she told herself. Of course he did not want a whore's daughter to be the mother of his heir. Of course he did not love her because no one, apart from her sister, ever had.

'You can't think of any reason to stay?' Kadir's jaw hardened when she shook her head. 'I thought you had enjoyed the days we spent together, and I know I gave you pleasure every night, just as you captivated me with your sensuality. We're good together, Lexi.'

Pride forced her chin up to meet his gaze. 'I don't deny we had some fun. But it didn't mean anything, did it? Now we know there is no baby it's time to move on.'

She was leaving him. Kadir's heart gave a painful jolt. In his mind he was seven years old, running down the palace steps after his mother, tears running down his face. *'Why do you have to go back to England, Mama? Why don't you want to stay here with me and Baba?'*

'I'll still see you, darling, when you come to stay at Montgomery Manor. But I don't belong in Zenhab. I can't live with the restrictions of being the wife of the Sultan.' Judith had bent down and kissed his cheek. Kadir still remembered the scent of the perfume she had worn that day. *'The truth is that I want to be free to live my own life.'*

Was that why Lexi had decided to leave him? Did she care more about her freedom and her career than him? 'I suppose you want to continue flying helicopters,' he said tersely.

'Yes, I love being a pilot.' Lexi made a show of checking her watch. 'Look, I really need to go if I'm going to catch my flight. You still have my passport,' she reminded him.

He was silent for a few moments before he gave a shrug. 'I'll tell Yusuf to bring it to you. The helicopter will take you to the airport but you'll have to wait while it's being refuelled.'

He moved suddenly and Lexi gave a startled cry when he pulled her cap off, freeing her hair so that it tumbled around her shoulders.

Kadir slid his hand beneath her chin and tilted her face up, subjecting her to an unsparing appraisal that took in the dark circles under her eyes and the tears sparkling on her lashes. A fierce emotion stirred inside him but he ruthlessly suppressed it.

'Goodbye, angel-face,' he murmured before he strode out of the room, leaving Lexi with the exotic scent of his cologne and a heart that felt as though it had splintered into a thousand shards.

Her plane was due to leave Zenhab's main airport in less than an hour, Lexi fretted. She had been delayed at the palace because apparently there had been a problem with the fuel pump for the helicopter, and once that had been sorted out she'd still had to wait for Yusuf, who had eventually appeared with her passport and a rambling explanation about how it had not been where he had thought it was and he had spent ages looking for it.

In half an hour it would be dark. She was used to the way the sun set quickly over the desert. Right now, the sun was a huge ball of fire that was turning the sea orange.

The sea!

Frowning, she turned to the helicopter pilot and spoke into her headset. 'Mitch, you're going the wrong way. The airport is in the opposite direction.'

'This is the direction I was told to fly. I'm just following the Sultan's orders.'

Below them, Lexi saw the black silhouettes of palm trees rising up from a desert island, and her heart gave a jolt as the chopper swooped lower over an empty beach. *Jinan.* 'Why have you brought me here?' she asked Mitch fiercely.

The pilot landed the chopper on the sand. 'This is where the Sultan told me to bring you.' Reaching under his seat, he handed her a jar of honey. 'He said to give you this.'

Thankfully, the fading light hid her scarlet face from the pilot. Memories of Kadir's unconventional use of honey when they had been trapped on the island flooded Lexi's mind. Was he playing some sort of cruel mind game with her? She made a muffled sound in her throat and curled her hand around the jar. 'It'll make a useful missile to throw at him,' she muttered.

'The Sultan said you'd probably say that.' Mitch grinned. 'It seems like Sultan Kadir knows you pretty well.'

What the devil was Kadir playing at? Lexi's heart was pounding as she marched up the beach. She scrambled over the sand dunes and saw the oasis and next to it the tent, illuminated by glowing lamps that cast shadows onto the canvas.

Pushing through the flaps, she stopped dead and stared at Kadir, sprawled on a pile of silk cushions. He was wearing a black robe tied loosely at the waist and revealing his bare chest. In the lamplight his body gleamed like polished bronze, and as he propped himself up on one elbow Lexi's eyes were drawn to his hard abdominal muscles and the line of dark hairs that arrowed lower. She remembered that the very first time she'd met him she had imagined the Sultan lying on silk cushions, beckoning to her to join him.

'Good, you brought the honey,' he drawled.

She gripped the heavy glass jar. 'Have you any idea what I'd like to do with this?'

'Show me,' he invited softly.

'Don't tempt me.'

'Why not?' He sat up and stared at her intently. 'You tempt me constantly. I think about you all the time.'

'Don't say things that aren't true.' She stared at the patterned rug on the floor, willing herself not to cry.

'I never took you for a coward, Lexi.'

'I'm not a coward, damn you.'

'Then look at me.'

Something in his voice, a tremor of emotion

that felt like an arrow through her heart, made her slowly raise her head. His eyes were darker than she had ever seen them—dark with pain, she realised with a jolt. His teasing smile had disappeared and he looked serious and tense, almost—*nervous*. But that was ridiculous. What did the powerful Sultan of Zenhab, the desert king, have to fear?

'You really would have gone back to England, wouldn't you?' he said harshly. 'After everything we shared, the most beautiful time of my life, I thought, hoped you were starting to trust me.'

He couldn't sound hurt, Lexi told herself. She must be imagining the raw expression in his eyes. 'You said it was for the best that I'm not pregnant.' Her voice shook. 'You said goodbye at the palace and let me go.' Only now did she acknowledge she had been testing him, hoping at the eleventh hour for a miracle.

'I was hurting,' he shocked her by saying, 'and I was angry with myself for failing to do enough to convince you that we have something special. I went into the gardens and sat on my father's favourite bench. Remembering how much he loved me, the confidence I gained from my happy childhood, made me understand why trust is such a difficult concept for you. I understand why you are scared of emotions because you were rejected by your birth mother and your adoptive parents failed to make you feel loved.'

He stood up and walked towards her, stealing Lexi's breath with his masculine beauty, his powerful body all satiny skin and strong muscles.

'I do think it is better that you didn't fall pregnant the last time we were on Jinan.' He tipped her face towards him when she tried to look away to hide her pain and confusion. 'I can't imagine you would be happy to have an accidental pregnancy after what you told me about your biological mother,' he said with an intuition that touched a chord inside Lexi. 'When you conceive my baby I hope it will be an event we have planned, and our child will be longed for and loved from the moment of conception.'

Her heart was thumping so hard she could barely breathe. 'I don't understand,' she whispered. 'Why did you bring me here?'

He brushed her hair back from her face with gentle fingers. 'Jinan is where it began, although that's not quite true because it started when you hauled me out of a stormy sea and promptly wiped the floor with me.' He smiled. 'No one had ever spoken to me like that before. I was furious but at the same time all I could think of was how badly I wanted to kiss you. But I knew I couldn't. I had to honour my arranged marriage, and my desire for you was forbidden.

'I thought I would have no trouble resisting you,' he said roughly. 'Ever since I was a young man, I had resigned myself to the prospect that I must marry for duty, not love. And in some strange way it was a relief to know I would not suffer the heartbreak my father felt when my mother left him. My emotions would never be at risk, or so I believed. But when the kidnapper threatened you with a gun the truth hit me like a bullet through my heart.'

Kadir closed his eyes for a few seconds, haunted by the memory of the fear that had churned in his stomach when he'd thought she might be killed.

'I realised that if I lost you, my life would not be worth living. I also knew that I could not keep the promise I had made my father and marry Haleema. I could not marry without love, even though my decision meant I might lose my kingdom and my role as Sultan of Zenhab.'

Lexi was stunned by his revelation. 'I know how much it would have hurt you to break your promise to your father. You loved him so much.' She did not know what to think, and she was afraid to trust the expression in Kadir's eyes. He had told her he'd realised he could not marry without love, but that didn't mean that he loved her.

For some reason she thought of her sister. Athena had always been patient and loving, never asking Lexi for anything in return. She felt ashamed that it had taken her so long to tell her sister she loved her.

She remembered the magical days she had spent with Kadir and knew she hadn't imagined their friendship that had grown stronger every day. He had been kind and caring, patient and *loving*, but she had listened to her insecurities and been afraid to listen to her heart. She *had* been a coward, Lexi acknowledged.

But a lifetime of feeling rejected was not easy to overcome, and her voice caught in her throat when she spoke. 'The days and nights we spent together while we waited to find out if I was pregnant were the most beautiful of my life too. I didn't want them to end but I knew they couldn't last and I was sure you couldn't feel anything for me.'

'Why couldn't I?' he demanded.

'You are the Sultan of Zenhab,' she said as if it explained everything, 'and my mother was a whore.'

'I don't give a damn if your mother is a Martian.' Kadir seized hold of her shoulders and stared down at her startled face. 'Will you marry me, Lexi Howard?'

She so desperately wanted to trust the fierce emotion blazing in his eyes. Her bravery had never been put to such a defining test, not even when she had risked her life flying rescue missions in war-torn Afghanistan.

'There's no reason for you to marry me,' she reminded him.

He moved his hands up to frame her face and captured the tears clinging to her eyelashes on his fingers. 'I love you, Lexi. That's the only reason why I want you to be my wife and the mother of my children that, fate willing, we will be blessed with in the future. I want you as my lover and my best friend, and I hope you will be my Queen and help me rule my kingdom.'

He could not catch all her tears as they slipped down her cheeks, and he tasted them on her lips when he covered her mouth with his and kissed her with such beguiling tenderness that Lexi's heart felt as though it would burst.

'I love you,' she whispered, and suddenly the words weren't hard to say because they came from her heart. She said them over and over in a husky litany that moved Kadir unbearably because he knew the demons she had faced and beaten to give him her trust.

He lifted her into his arms and carried her over to the pile of silk cushions, where he removed her skirt and blouse with hands that visibly shook. 'I will tell you every day for the rest of our lives how much I love you,' he promised. 'You are my heart's desire, the love of my life, *habibi*.'

From somewhere he produced a small box, which he opened to reveal an exquisite oval blue diamond ring.

'I knew the colour would be a perfect match for your eyes. Blue diamonds are rare and precious, just as you are to me, my angel.' He looked intently into Lexi's eyes. 'You haven't given me an answer. Will you make me the happiest man in the world and marry me? Will you love me for eternity, as I will love you?'

Lexi wiped away her tears and met his gaze, her blue eyes sparkling as bright as the diamond he slid on her finger. 'Yes, my Sultan, my love. I never knew I could feel this happy,' she whispered, shivering with anticipation as he removed her underwear and knelt over her.

'Tomorrow we'll start planning our wedding,' he promised. 'Luca De Rossi guessed how I felt about you when we stayed at his villa in Italy, and he will be my best man. Who will you choose for your chief bridesmaid?'

'My sister,' Lexi said instantly. 'Athena suggested I should tell you I love you.'

'Why don't you show me?' Kadir murmured.

'With pleasure, my Sultan.' She took him by surprise, pushing him back against the cushions and straddling him at the same time as she unscrewed the lid of the jar of honey.

'*Habibi*…where are you going to pour that honey?'

Kadir groaned when she showed him.

* * * * *

LARGER-PRINT BOOKS!
GET 2 FREE LARGER-PRINT NOVELS PLUS
2 FREE GIFTS!

HARLEQUIN®

I N T R I G U E
BREATHTAKING ROMANTIC SUSPENSE

YES! Please send me 2 FREE LARGER-PRINT Harlequin® Intrigue novels and my 2 FREE gifts (gifts are worth about $10). After receiving them, if I don't wish to receive any more books, I can return the shipping statement marked "cancel." If I don't cancel, I will receive 6 brand-new novels every month and be billed just $5.49 per book in the U.S. or $6.24 per book in Canada. That's a saving of at least 11% off the cover price! It's quite a bargain! Shipping and handling is just 50¢ per book in the U.S. and 75¢ per book in Canada.* I understand that accepting the 2 free books and gifts places me under no obligation to buy anything. I can always return a shipment and cancel at any time. Even if I never buy another book, the two free books and gifts are mine to keep forever.

199/399 HDN GHWN

Name	(PLEASE PRINT)	
Address		Apt. #
City	State/Prov.	Zip/Postal Code

Signature (if under 18, a parent or guardian must sign)

Mail to the **Reader Service**:
IN U.S.A.: P.O. Box 1867, Buffalo, NY 14240-1867
IN CANADA: P.O. Box 609, Fort Erie, Ontario L2A 5X3

Are you a subscriber to Harlequin® Intrigue books
and want to receive the larger-print edition?
Call 1-800-873-8635 today or visit www.ReaderService.com.

* Terms and prices subject to change without notice. Prices do not include applicable taxes. Sales tax applicable in N.Y. Canadian residents will be charged applicable taxes. Offer not valid in Quebec. This offer is limited to one order per household. Not valid for current subscribers to Harlequin Intrigue Larger-Print books. All orders subject to credit approval. Credit or debit balances in a customer's account(s) may be offset by any other outstanding balance owed by or to the customer. Please allow 4 to 6 weeks for delivery. Offer available while quantities last.

Your Privacy—The Reader Service is committed to protecting your privacy. Our Privacy Policy is available online at www.ReaderService.com or upon request from the Reader Service.

We make a portion of our mailing list available to reputable third parties that offer products we believe may interest you. If you prefer that we not exchange your name with third parties, or if you wish to clarify or modify your communication preferences, please visit us at www.ReaderService.com/consumerschoice or write to us at Reader Service Preference Service, P.O. Box 9062, Buffalo, NY 14240-9062. Include your complete name and address.

LARGER-PRINT BOOKS!
GET 2 FREE LARGER-PRINT NOVELS PLUS
2 FREE GIFTS!

HARLEQUIN®

Romance

From the Heart, For the Heart

YES! Please send me 2 FREE LARGER-PRINT Harlequin® Romance novels and my 2 FREE gifts (gifts are worth about $10). After receiving them, if I don't wish to receive any more books, I can return the shipping statement marked "cancel." If I don't cancel, I will receive 4 brand-new novels every month and be billed just $5.09 per book in the U.S. or $5.49 per book in Canada. That's a savings of at least 15% off the cover price! It's quite a bargain! Shipping and handling is just 50¢ per book in the U.S. and 75¢ per book in Canada.* I understand that accepting the 2 free books and gifts places me under no obligation to buy anything. I can always return a shipment and cancel at any time. Even if I never buy another book, the two free books and gifts are mine to keep forever.

119/319 HDN GHWC

Name _____ (PLEASE PRINT)

Address _____ Apt. #

City _____ State/Prov. _____ Zip/Postal Code

Signature (if under 18, a parent or guardian must sign)

Mail to the Reader Service:
IN U.S.A.: P.O. Box 1867, Buffalo, NY 14240-1867
IN CANADA: P.O. Box 609, Fort Erie, Ontario L2A 5X3
Want to try two free books from another line?
Call 1-800-873-8635 or visit www.ReaderService.com.

* Terms and prices subject to change without notice. Prices do not include applicable taxes. Sales tax applicable in N.Y. Canadian residents will be charged applicable taxes. Offer not valid in Quebec. This offer is limited to one order per household. Not valid for current subscribers to Harlequin Romance Larger-Print books. All orders subject to credit approval. Credit or debit balances in a customer's account(s) may be offset by any other outstanding balance owed by or to the customer. Please allow 4 to 6 weeks for delivery. Offer available while quantities last.

Your Privacy—The Reader Service is committed to protecting your privacy. Our Privacy Policy is available online at www.ReaderService.com or upon request from the Reader Service.

We make a portion of our mailing list available to reputable third parties that offer products we believe may interest you. If you prefer that we not exchange your name with third parties, or if you wish to clarify or modify your communication preferences, please visit us at www.ReaderService.com/consumerschoice or write to us at Reader Service Preference Service, P.O. Box 9062, Buffalo, NY 14240-9062. Include your complete name and address.

HRLP15